MW00453860

Seabreeze Inn and Coral Cottage series

"A wonderful story... Will make you feel like the sea breeze is streaming through your hair." – Laura Bradbury, Bestselling Author

"A novel that gives fans of romantic sagas a compelling voice to follow." – *Booklist*

"An entertaining beach read with multi-generational context and humor." – *InD'Tale* Magazine

"Wonderful characters and a sweet story." – Kellie Coates Gilbert, Bestselling Author

"A fun read that grabs you at the start." – Tina Sloan, Author and Award-Winning Actress

"Jan Moran is the queen of the epic romance." —Rebecca Forster, *USA Today* Bestselling Author

"The women are intelligent and strong. At the core is a strong, close-knit family." — Betty's Reviews

The Chocolatier

"A delicious novel, makes you long for chocolate." – *Ciao Tutti*

"Smoothly written...full of intrigue, love, secrets, and romance." – *Lekker Lezen*

The Winemakers

"Readers will devour this page-turner as the mystery and passions spin out." – *Library Journal*

"As she did in *Scent of Triumph*, Moran weaves knowledge of wine and winemaking into this intense family drama." – *Booklist*

The Perfumer: Scent of Triumph

"Heartbreaking, evocative, and inspiring, this book is a powerful journey." – Allison Pataki, *NYT* Bestselling Author of *The Accidental Empress*

"A sweeping saga of one woman's journey through World War II and her unwillingness to give up even when faced with the toughest challenges." — Anita Abriel, Author of *The Light After the War*

"A captivating tale of love, determination and reinvention." — Karen Marin, Givenchy Paris

"A stylish, compelling story of a family. What sets this apart is the backdrop of perfumery that suffuses the story with the delicious aromas – a remarkable feat!" — Liz Trenow, *NYT* Bestselling Author of *The Forgotten Seamstress*

BOOKS BY JAN MORAN

Coral Cottage Series

Coral Cottage

Coral Cafe

Coral Holiday

Coral Weddings

Coral Celebration

Coral Memories

Summer Beach Series

Seabreeze Inn

Seabreeze Summer

Seabreeze Sunset

Seabreeze Christmas

Seabreeze Wedding

Seabreeze Book Club

Seabreeze Shores

Seabreeze Reunion

Seabreeze Gala

USA TODAY BESTSELLING AUTHOR

JAN MORAN

Coral
CELEBRATION

THE CORAL COTTAGE AT SUMMER BEACH
BOOK FIVE

CORAL CELEBRATION

CORAL COTTAGE AT SUMMER BEACH SERIES
BOOK 5

JAN MORAN

SUNNY PALMS

PRESS

Copyright © 2023 Jan Moran. All Rights Reserved.

All rights reserved under International and Pan-American Copyright Conventions, including the right of reproduction in whole or in part in any form or by any electronic or mechanical means including information storage and retrieval systems, without written permission, except in the case of brief quotations embodied in critical articles and reviews.

Library of Congress Cataloging-in-Publication Data
Moran, Jan.
/ by Jan Moran

ISBN 978-1-64778-133-0 (ebook)
ISBN 978-1-64778-134-7 (paperback)
ISBN 978-1-64778-135-4 (hardcover)
ISBN 978-1-64778-136-1 (large print)
ISBN 978-1-64778-137-8 (audiobook)

Published by Sunny Palms Press. Cover design by Sleepy Fox Studios. Cover images copyright Deposit Photos.

Sunny Palms Press
9663 Santa Monica Blvd STE 1158
Beverly Hills, CA 90210 USA
www.JanMoran.com

For all who enjoy visiting the world of Summer Beach.
Thank you for reading!

Receive a complimentary Summer Beach Welcome Kit by downloading
an ebook or printable PDF from:
www.JanMoran.com/SummerBeachWelcomeKit

1

"Order up," Marina called to her daughter, who was waiting tables on the sunny patio with the beach view.

She added a drizzle of raspberry vinaigrette to the spinach salads she had prepared with scoops of berries, sprinkles of feta cheese, and glazed walnuts. This dish had become a popular summer special at the Coral Cafe.

Heather sailed into the kitchen to pick up the order. "Sounds like the centennial celebration is out of control. There's a mutiny going on at table five."

Marina gave her a warning look. "What did I tell you about gossiping?"

"I call it being well informed," Heather said, winking at Cruise, who was flipping turkey burgers on the cooktop.

Marina glanced up from her open-air kitchen workspace, concerned about the important Summer Beach event, which was the major tourist event of the summer this year. The small town had been incorporated a hundred years ago, and residents were eager to celebrate.

Peering out onto the dining patio, Marina saw volunteers huddled around a table under a broad coral umbrella. "What's going on out there?"

"The committee is voting to replace Rhoda, who didn't show up to today's meeting," Heather replied, lowering her voice. "Or the last one. I heard them say she has barely organized the parade. But no one else wants to take on that responsibility."

"Rhoda's mind is probably elsewhere." Marina had heard that Rhoda's mother was having health challenges. That had to be weighing on the poor woman, but she didn't strike Marina as well organized anyway. "I'm sure they'll sort it out."

Heather picked up the salads. "You'd have that organized in no time, Mom. Look what you've done with this place."

"I offered to bring the food truck. I'll reach out again after our trip."

Marina was also growing concerned for the community and the event. She had left messages for Rhoda expressing interest in bringing her Coral Cafe food truck to the event, but the other woman hadn't returned her calls. Neither had she been in touch with other restaurants. They would all need time to arrange staffing, menus, and supplies, and the event was only a few weeks away now.

No wonder people were growing nervous. The Summer Beach Centennial promotions were running all over Southern California, and a sizable number of visitors were expected. All the inns had been fully booked for weeks.

Marina would certainly be prepared at the cafe, but she had hoped to bring her food truck to the event venue at the beach. She clicked her tongue, wondering who they would find to oversee efforts on such short notice.

She would mention that to Ginger, she decided. Her grandmother knew everyone in town.

As for Marina, she had other things on her mind. Jack was at home packing the VW van for the short getaway they had planned. This was her first break since the spring rush kicked off the busy tourist season. They were leaving early in the morning and would only be gone a couple of nights, but it would be well worth it.

She turned to Cruise, who was placing fresh sweet potato fries into sizzling hot oil. With his tattoos and sun-bleached hair wound into a man-bun at the nap of his neck, he was young and had plenty of energy.

"I left a checklist in the prep area for you."

"Don't worry, I've got this." Cruise slapped more turkey patties on the grill for the popular sliders.

"I'm sure you do, but I'd still like for you to review it," she said evenly.

Cruise was talented, but sometimes he made assumptions or took shortcuts she had to correct. Still, she liked him well enough, and so did Heather. He was here only for the summer, working part-time for her and surfing as much as he could.

Her sister Brooke would wait tables, and their grandmother Ginger would greet customers and oversee the cafe, but still, Marina worried. Although the cafe was going well, one slip-up could tarnish its reputation and damage the business. She had worked hard to create systems that others could follow to ensure consistency.

Otherwise, she would have no life outside of work. She had little as it was.

Heather returned to the kitchen and clipped another order to the rotating rack. "Those fries sure smell good, Cruise. Will you save some for me?"

"Always," he replied with a grin. "With my special garlic aioli."

Heather beamed at him. "You're the best."

He puffed out his chest. "I like to think so."

Heather laughed and popped him with her dishtowel. "Oh, listen to you."

Chuckling, Cruise jumped back, hitting the handle of a hot skillet.

"Hey, you two," Marina said. "Careful round fires and knives. We can't afford any accidents."

"Sorry, Mom." Heather picked up an order and ducked from the kitchen, grinning back at Cruise.

This interaction caught Marina's attention. Heather and Cruise had become good friends. That was all it was, she thought, although Heather hadn't talked about seeing anyone else this summer. Usually, her daughter confided in her.

Marina blew a wisp of hair from her eyes. Maybe she worried too much, but it was a habit she'd developed after Stan's death when she was raising her twins.

Now in her mid-forties with a new husband she adored, it was time to eliminate habits that no longer served her. By tomorrow morning, she would be on the open road with him and their children—except for Ethan, who was on the golf course with clients.

With Jack by her side and a new future ahead, it was time to open her heart and clear her mind. As she worked on another order, she smiled to herself. Two days in nature was just what she needed.

As Jack steered his retro VW van, Marina leaned back in her seat, taking in the ocean view. The day was sunny, so she'd worn denim shorts with a white T-shirt, and she felt almost like a kid again, shedding the stress she'd been under for months.

Heather and Leo were in the back seat with Scout stretched between them, his tail wagging as he pawed for belly rubs.

This was a short break they had all needed.

"Keep an eye on the ocean," Jack said as he wound along the narrow beach access road. "We might see some whales migrating."

Leo pressed his hands to the window. "What kind of whales, Dad?"

When Jack didn't reply, Heather tousled her younger stepbrother's shaggy hair. "It's summer, so that means finbacks and blue whales."

Jack grinned. "I'm impressed."

"So am I," Marina said. "Where did you learn that?"

Heather shrugged off the compliments. "Just random facts I pick up at the cafe. You'd be surprised what you learn by listening. Like the centennial mutiny yesterday. I'm amazed that people still think the help can't hear."

"Why not?" Leo asked with the wide eyes of a pre-teen. "You have ears."

They all laughed at that, and Heather smiled at him. "It's a saying, but it's still true. People forget that servers can hear the secrets they share."

Jack shot Marina a look of concern. "What's this about a mutiny?"

"The committee voted to oust Rhoda," Marina replied. "At the moment, no one is in charge of the centennial volunteer committee."

"You and Ginger could sort that out," Jack said.

"Not you, too." Marina laughed as Heather poked her.

As good as life was in Summer Beach, the summer season was a marathon at the cafe. She had to pace herself to avoid burnout.

She was glad to have her daughter helping at the cafe. Heather was on summer break from the university. Last year, she had an internship, but this year, she'd opted to stay in Summer Beach, saying she wanted to spend a summer at home before she graduated and got a job that would probably take her elsewhere.

Once again, Marina would miss her.

After Marina's news anchor position ended disastrously, she had closed her flat in San Francisco and moved to Summer Beach. At the time, the twins were attending Duke University on the East Coast.

Ethan was there on a golf scholarship, yet he struggled academically due to dyslexia. After he left school and landed a job at a golf country club in San Diego, Heather no longer wanted to stay in North Carolina alone. With Ethan on the path to turn pro in golf, Heather joined the family in Summer Beach to finish school in San Diego.

Jack rotated his neck and drew a hand over it, winching.

"Need a break from driving?" Marina reached over to massage his neck and shoulders. "Wow, you have some ferocious knots."

"Right there, thanks for that," he replied, softly squeezing her knee. "When we find a place to stop, we'll have that picnic you packed. Just a little longer."

She placed her hand on his. Marina was growing more comfortable with Jack every day, and she enjoyed the small touches and conversations that made up their daily lives. Their first anniversary was coming up soon.

In their first year, they both had to adjust to new routines. Initially, Jack had been shocked when Leo landed in his life. He'd gone from being single, living in New York City, and working as an investigative reporter to being a new, inexperienced father in a quiet, Southern California beach town.

While Jack had adapted, he also confided in Marina about the weight of his new role and responsibilities to his son, who would soon enter middle school in the sixth grade. This was a critical time for a young boy, and Jack didn't want to make any more mistakes than he already had.

From the corner of her eye, she saw Jack stifle a yawn. Add a first marriage in his forties to the mix, and Marina understood why Jack had trouble sleeping.

"We should stop soon," she said. "No need to push on."

"Okay. As soon as I find a good spot.' He rubbed his eyes and stared ahead.

"How are your illustrations for the new book coming along?" she asked, making conversation to keep him alert. Jack had been working hard on a set of illustrations for her grandmother's surprisingly popular children's book series.

"Pretty well," he replied. "Ginger is an excellent collaborator. Bringing her stories to life is a nice change from the big city grind."

"That article seems to be taking longer than you expected."

He shook his head. "One lead often leads to five. I need to follow them all."

Jack was also writing a lengthy investigative article for his former editor in New York. Having won a Pulitzer Prize, Jack was well respected in his field. He had taken on new assignments because he was concerned about the cost of Leo's education.

Marina understood his need to meet the new challenges of fatherhood. He had also bought the beach bungalow he'd been renting. She shared the expenses with her earnings from the cafe.

Marina was proud of Jack, and he was equally pleased about her cafe and food truck, though finding time for each other was challenging. Hence, this short getaway for their new blended family.

Suddenly, something caught Marina's attention. "Slow down," she cried in alarm, peering out the window. "Something washed up on the beach. We need to turn around."

Jack grimaced. "Is it dead or alive?"

"Oh, wait. I see it, Mom." Heather flipped her wavy, dark blond ponytail and twisted in her seat. "Looks sort of lumpy."

"I think it's a fishing net," Marina said, squinting against the sun. "But it's moving. An animal might be trapped in it."

"Like a dolphin?" Leo asked, looking worried.

At that, Heather leaned forward and tapped Jack. "We really need to stop."

"Will do." Jack looked back at Leo. "Hey, son. Will you keep an eye on Scout? We don't need him barking at whatever creature is in trouble while we check it out. Can you manage that?"

"Sure, Dad." Leo ran his hand over the yellow Labrador retriever, and Scout nudged him with his snout, his mouth stretched into a panting grin.

With his thick dark hair and bright blue eyes, Leo was a younger replica of his father. At eleven, Leo was becoming more responsible, and Marina was pleased that he'd accepted his father's marriage—and her as his stepmother. Ethan was also coaching the young boy in golf while he worked toward his dream of turning pro.

While her children liked Jack, he seemed a little unsure

of his role with Heather and Ethan. Getting married was one thing. Becoming a family was another.

Jack waited for a car to pass before executing a U-turn. "Where exactly is this sea creature from the depths of the ocean?"

"On the other side of that outcropping of rocks." Marina pointed at a spot near the shoreline. "See it now?"

"Yeah, I do." He pulled to the shoulder of the road. "I've got a knife in the back. I can try to free whatever it is." He flipped on the emergency flashers. "Could be another nosy dog. Leo, put the leash on Scout and keep a strong grip on him."

"I'll help him," Heather said, sliding on her flip-flops.

They got out of the van and walked cautiously toward the shifting mound of heavy netting by the water's edge.

When Marina saw what it was, her heart leapt. "They're young sea lions. More than one."

"Are you sure they're not seals?" Jack asked, approaching them.

Marina stood near the bundle, careful to keep her distance. "See their flippers and how they can walk on them? Plus, they have snouts like dogs."

She knew humans shouldn't touch marine mammals unless they knew what they were doing, and she certainly didn't.

"Oh no, one of them looks hurt," Heather said, pressing a hand to her chest. "We can't release them like that. They need help."

"There might be a mammal rescue group in the vicinity." Marina looked at her phone, and her heart sank. "I don't have a signal."

Suddenly, a loud, strangled bark erupted behind them.

Marina whipped around. Judging from the distress in the

animal's voice, she said, "I think that's the mother. Or father. We should stay back."

"Poor Mama," Heather said. "I wish we could give her babies back right now."

"Hold onto Scout," Jack said, backing away.

The larger sea lion seemed to sense they meant no harm, but it continued to pace in distress. Marina breathed out a guarded sigh of relief.

As they were retreating from the net, Heather cried, "I have a signal."

"Quick, search for a number for ocean mammal rescue," Marina said. "And don't move from that spot."

Heather tapped the screen a few times. "I think I've got it. But I don't know where we are."

"Tap the arrow on a map," Leo said, his arms wrapped around Scout. "That locates you."

"How do you know that?" Jack asked, clearly impressed.

Leo grinned. "I saw it on a video."

Heather handed the phone to Marina. "Mom, would you talk to them?"

"Sure." Marina looked at the screen. Heather had pulled up a hotline number for a marine mammal rescue. "Jack, would you keep an eye on the mother and the pups?"

"Here goes." Marina tapped the number and told the person who answered where they were and what they'd found.

After she hung up, Jack asked, "How soon can they come?"

"They're about ten minutes away," Marina replied. "They said not to approach or try to help them. With one of the pups injured, it could make the mother angry. They're usually not dangerous, but sea lions will defend their young."

They waited, keeping watch over the young sea lion

family. Soon, a blue, four-wheel-drive truck emblazoned with a bright yellow logo pulled onto the beach.

A team of several women and men jumped out. The tallest one, a good-looking young man with closely cropped hair and a good physique, seemed to be in charge.

He had an easy, genuine smile that Marina immediately liked.

"I'm Blake Hayes," he said. "We appreciate your call. We see this more than we'd like. My team can cut the net, but since one is injured, we'll take them all to our center for observation."

"What do you think happened?" Heather asked.

Blake glanced at his team, who were assessing the situation. "Sea lions and others get caught in fishing nets, and the tide washes them in. That's probably the mother over there. She must have followed her pups, trying to save them. She looks exhausted, too. It's a good thing you called."

Heather tucked a strand of hair behind her ear. "Well, actually, it was my mom."

"But Heather insisted we stop," Marina said.

A smile touched Blake's face. "I'm glad you did. Heather, it's nice to meet you."

One of Blake's colleagues raised a hand. "Hey, Dr. Blake, you need to look at this little guy."

"Excuse me," he said to Heather. "It's nice to meet you and your family."

"Should we stay?" Heather asked.

"You don't have to, but you can." Blake reached into his pocket. "If you see any other stranded marine mammals, here's my card. Do you live around here?"

"In Summer Beach," Heather replied.

"Nice village." Blake smiled. "This won't take long." He trotted toward his team.

Scout strained against Leo, and Jack took over. "Thanks, sport. I got him now."

Marina put her arm around Heather. "You did a good thing by asking Jack to pull over. That shows your kind heart."

Watching Blake and his team, Heather shrugged. "Wouldn't anyone do that?"

"You'd be surprised." Marina stood with her family, and they continued watching the team work to free the family of sea lions.

After inspecting the injured pup and administering first aid, Blake helped the team load the young sea lion into the truck. Shortly, another vehicle pulled up.

Blake walked back to Marina and the others. "I wanted to thank you again. We'll take them all in for treatment, but they'll probably be fit to release soon. If you hadn't called, they might have perished. This is a lonely stretch of the beach, especially during the week." He looked at Heather. "Do you want me to let you know when we release them?"

"I'd like that," Heather said shyly. "You can find me at the Coral Cafe in Summer Beach. It's my mom's restaurant."

"Actually, I've been there," Blake said, raising his brow. "It's very good."

"Are you a sea lion doctor?" Leo asked.

Blake knelt to Leo's height. "I'm an aquatic veterinarian. Ever since I was your age, I wanted to help animals that make their home in the sea."

"That's cool," Leo said, eyeing the truck. "And you get to drive that?"

"Sure do," Blake replied. "Come by the center some-time. I'll give you a ride and show you around. We have a full medical facility for marine mammals. Around here, it's mostly sea lions, seals, and turtles, but we help all sorts."

Leo's eyes widened. "Even whales?"

"You bet." Blake chuckled. "I've treated whales and sent them back to live in the sea."

After Blake and his team left, Jack led Scout to the car, and everyone piled in. They drove a short distance and stopped for their picnic. Marina opened the back of the VW, which had a small built-in kitchen. With Heather's help, she began to assemble sandwiches.

"What an adventure that was," Marina said. "I'm glad we could help."

Heather gazed toward the ocean. "I wonder what it's like to spend your days working around animals?"

"I think it would take a compassionate soul to do that," Marina replied.

Heather tore off crisp lettuce leaves for the sandwiches. "Do you still need help for the anniversary party Ginger arranged this weekend?"

With her connections, Marina's grandmother brought in a lot of business for the cafe and the food truck she'd added. Ginger's friends had booked the food truck for a party at their beach house.

"If you're available, I could use you." Thinking about how Heather had looked at Blake, Marina wondered if she was interested in anyone. She hadn't dated much since she'd returned from North Carolina, but Heather was naturally reserved. She had a history of anxiety about tests in school. "But anytime you have a date, let me know. I can cover for you."

Heather shrugged. "You have Jack and Leo to think about now."

"Your life is important, too. I'm thinking of hiring another server." She paused. "Dr. Blake seemed nice."

A swift, shy smile crossed Heather's face, giving her away. "He's older than I am."

"Probably only a few years." Once again, Marina had the sense that Heather was holding something back. "Have you met someone at school?"

"Nope, no one."

Heather was quick to answer, Marina thought. But with Jack looking hungry and Leo racing toward them with Scout, she let it go for now.

As she was slicing the sandwiches, her phone buzzed in her pocket. Thinking it might be someone at the cafe, she asked Heather to finish and pulled out her phone.

Her hands were slippery, and she fumbled with the screen, jabbing at it with her knuckles. "Hello?"

"Marina, I'm so glad I caught you," Rhoda said, sounding out of breath.

At once, Marina's heart sank upon hearing Rhoda's voice. Of all the people she'd met in Summer Beach, Rhoda was one of the more challenging locals. Whenever she called, it was to ask for a personal favor or help with something. Once, she had asked Marina to comp a fancy lunch for thirty of her friends, supposedly to introduce them to the cafe.

However, Marina knew one of those friends who told her it was Rhoda's birthday. Rhoda had been huffy when Marina declined, citing the inability to host such a large party for free. Otherwise, she'd be comping everyone's birthday party in Summer Beach.

"Hi, Rhoda," Marina said, trying to sound pleasantly rushed. "I'm not at the cafe today. Jack and I have taken the kids for a holiday, so I really can't talk. But I hope your mother is feeling better."

"A little, thanks. I need to talk to you, and this will only take a minute if you say yes." Rhoda's voice was edged with desperation. "I need you to step up for the centennial celebration."

"Of course," Marina said, wondering if Rhoda was still in charge. "I'm happy to bring the food truck downtown for the parade."

"Okay, but I'm not calling about that. I've been trying to organize everything, but it's too much for one person. Then I thought about you. How you manage the cafe is amazing. Why, I never thought you could make a go of it, but you're still in business, even if you're not making much money."

Rhoda was also an expert at the back-handed compliment. Marina fought to maintain civility. "While I appreciate your point of view—"

"Please hear me out," Rhoda said, cutting her off. "You're the only person who hasn't turned me down, so you're my last hope. I thought I could do this myself, but no one is willing to step up to help."

"Don't you have a committee of volunteers?"

"They're no help."

Marina suppressed a groan. She could have predicted this. Ever since the announcement of the centennial celebration parade and fireworks, the mayor had been looking for someone to take charge. Rhoda lobbied hard for it. Marina suspected she liked feeling important, but her organizational skills were chaotic at best.

This was one mess Marina had to avoid. Jack and Heather were staring at her, listening to her side of the conversation. She owed it to them to stay out of this, too.

Marina faced the ocean breeze and ran a hand through

her hair. "Between the cafe and my family commitments, I hope you'll understand that I have to decline."

Rhoda seemed to pick up on Marina's hesitation. "You know, I've helped make your cafe the success that it is."

Here she goes, Marina thought, bracing herself. "Really? I don't see you there much." She refrained from adding that Rhoda had missed the last meeting at the cafe.

"Maybe not, but I've told hundreds, maybe thousands, of people about it. I'm practically a one-person PR firm for you. I won't say you owe me—I'm too classy for that—but with you on board, the centennial will be a guaranteed success. This time, I won't take no for an answer." Rhoda paused, lowering her voice as if for dramatic effect. "I know you're the person for the job. I even had a dream about it."

This was far too much for Marina. While the thought of volunteering for the centennial celebration was appealing, working closely with Rhoda was not. Maybe she meant well —and that was being generous—but she was a talkative whirlwind with little follow-through.

Still, Rhoda gossiped, and Marina didn't need her to start spreading rumors about the cafe.

"What a shame my life is so busy right now," Marina began, choosing her words carefully. "While I can't commit to helping you with planning and execution, I will bring my food truck to the event with a special menu. That's the best I can do, I'm afraid."

There was a pause on the other end of the line. "Well, that's something," Rhoda finally said, sounding deflated. "But I still need your help. Think about it, and I'll call you tomorrow."

Marina's gaze settled on Heather, who was finishing the lunch preparations. She thought of the life she had built in Summer Beach, and while she loved her community, working with Rhoda would be a disaster. And it sounded like the committee was replacing her anyway.

"You don't need to do that," Marina said, remaining firm in her decision. "I'm doing what I can for you. My food truck will be there. But you'll need someone else to help you with the event."

Rhoda heaved a sigh. "I've done a lot for you, but maybe you don't realize it. I've even invited a food critic to the Coral Cafe for you. He'll be showing up soon." She paused for a dramatic sigh. "Everyone I've talked to has said you're the perfect person to help me. I would hate for them to think badly of you or the cafe for not being willing to help me when I needed you. So, if you change your mind, you know where to find me."

Click.

Marina hung up and threw up her hands. "I shouldn't have taken that call."

"Bravo for sticking to your principles," Jack said, grinning. "She has some nerve. That last bit sounded like a mob boss. She tried every trick in the book."

"Could you hear what she was saying?" Marina asked.

"She's not shy, Mom." Heather giggled. "And somehow, you turned on your speakerphone. I almost cracked up when she started in on the dream."

Marina had to laugh at the absurdity of it all. "The funny thing is, if it weren't for her, working on the centennial celebration sounds like a lot of fun."

Heather put up the sandwiches, and Leo charged toward the lunch spread.

Jack scooped a sandwich onto a plate for Leo. "Let someone else take on that misery."

"I agree," Marina said as she wrapped the extra bread. "But I hope the centennial celebration won't be one of

Rhoda's more memorable disasters. Summer Beach deserves better than that."

Jack swept his arms around her and tapped her nose. "You don't have to solve other people's problems. Let the mayor figure it out."

2

*A*fter returning from their camping trip, the next few days flew past. On Saturday, Marina spent the afternoon after the lunch rush preparing for the anniversary beach party Ginger's friends were having.

Jack had left on a weekend fishing trip with a friend he was meeting from Los Angeles, and Leo was with his mother, so Marina would be on her own tonight anyway. The couple had also hired her sister Kai and her husband Axe to sing.

Marina loaded her food truck, which she'd affectionately nicknamed Coralina, with an Italian-themed menu for the fiftieth wedding anniversary of Ginger's friends, Valerie and Alan. When Marina and her team arrived at their home, Cruise parked the truck on one side of the property by the patio and near the beach.

With Heather serving, Marina and Cruise swung into action in the small kitchen, turning out crusty bread with antipasti and salads followed by lasagna and tiramisu. The food was well received, and the party was a huge success for Ginger's friends.

Among those friends was Rhoda. So far, Marina had succeeded in avoiding her.

While Kai and Axe entertained, Marina scooped out the dessert. "That's the last of the tiramisu." She covered the empty dish and set it aside to wash when they returned.

"Did you save some for Kai and Axe?" Heather asked.

Marina nodded toward a few smaller serving dishes. "I made extra, right over there. One for you, too. Let's take the rest of these to the buffet table."

"Aunt Kai sure sounds great tonight," Heather said. "I wish I had a natural talent like that."

"You have many other talents. And maybe some you haven't even discovered yet."

"Aren't talents things you're born with?"

"Not necessarily," Marina replied. "When you and Ethan left for school, I had no idea I'd be running a cafe within the year."

Heather smiled. "I was proud of you when you were on TV with the news, but that was only a job. You built the cafe from the ground up."

"With your help," Marina said. "And the rest of the family."

Finishing a song, Kai hit a high note, and the crowd applauded. She had dressed the part tonight in a glittery 1950s dress with a sweetheart neckline and a full skirt. Her strawberry blond hair was wound into a sleek chignon. When she began singing Doris Day's big hit, *Que Sera Sera*, couples filled the patio dance floor, swaying to the tune.

Marina loved listening to Kai. She was proud of her sister's achievements as a touring musical theater performer, and Kai and Axe's work at their new Seashell Amphitheater was paying off, too.

Heather watched, mesmerized as so many others were, too. Marina hoped her daughter would find a path she loved as much as Kai did.

The moon was high, but the party showed few signs of slowing down. "We should clean up," Marina said. She and Heather started back to the food truck.

"I love listening to Aunt Kai," Heather said, watching couples waltz gracefully across the patio under the stars. "That was beautiful music back then."

Cruise looked up from his work and grinned. "I thought you were a Swiftie."

"Nothing says I can't like Taylor Swift *and* the oldies." Heather lifted her chin. "I grew up listening to Ginger spinning Doris Day and Patsy Cline records on an old built-in record player she had in the family room."

"I remember," Marina said, smiling. "And that old turntable still works. Your grandmother has an amazing collection of vintage records. That music was before my time, too, but it's still wonderful."

"See?" Heather bumped Cruise's shoulder.

As if sensing they were talking about her, Ginger strode toward them. "You all look like you're up to no good."

"We were just talking about your record collection and how good this music is." Heather nodded toward the crowded dance floor. "These songs are making everyone feel young again."

"You're never too old to feel young." Ginger snapped her fingers to an Elvis tune that Axe was singing, complete with twisty dance moves. The crowd cheered on his antics.

Marina gazed at her grandmother with admiration. "I

don't know what your secret is, but I think you're aging backward."

"I like to think so," Ginger said. "It's all in the mind, my dear. At a certain age, you'll realize you once took life far too seriously." She gave Marina a pointed look.

"I've had my reasons. Times two," Marina added, putting her arm around Heather.

Raising twins by herself after Stan died had been overwhelming. If not for Ginger, she didn't know how she would have made it through that first year. She owed her grandmother so much.

"But this is now," Ginger replied, smiling at an older, well-dressed man approaching them. "It's time to lighten up."

As the music changed and Axe segued into Frank Sinatra's *Beyond the Sea*, a man Marina recognized from the cafe took Ginger's hand and whisked her away. Her floral skirt and scarf fluttered in the soft ocean breeze.

Heather grinned. "She doesn't just give advice, she lives it."

"Go, Ginger," Kai called out on the microphone, and everyone applauded. With the final set almost over, she took a bow when the song ended and stepped down.

Marina didn't know who was having more fun—the anniversary couple and their friends, Kai and Axe, or her crew at the food truck.

But that feeling was short-lived when Marina looked up and saw Rhoda charging toward her. She wore a sequined red dress that was hard to miss.

Sure enough, Rhoda had an air of urgency about her. "Have you changed your mind about helping me with the centennial celebration?"

Marina stiffened. "As you can see, I often work late." She gestured to the food truck.

Rhoda blew out a breath of exasperation. "Marina, I know I can be overwhelming, but it's only because this means so much to me and Summer Beach. Please tell me you'll help. I don't know what I'll do otherwise."

Marina's thoughts reeled back to their last conversation. While the centennial was important to the community, she couldn't handle Rhoda's mercurial personality or unpredictability. Yet, seeing the desperation in Rhoda's eyes, she felt a pang of guilt.

Feeling Heather's eyes on her, Marina said, "I gave you my answer. I will bring the food truck, but that's all I can do."

Rhoda's voice softened. "I promise, this time will be different. And I meant that about sending the food critic to the cafe."

"I wish you wouldn't." She didn't want to owe Rhoda any favors. Plus, she had plenty of business now, and critics could be risky. "My answer is still no."

Rhoda heaved a sigh and, after giving Marina a look of disgust, returned to the party.

"I was worried you might give in," Heather said, smiling. "Way to stand up to her, Mom."

"Someone has to manage the centennial, but it's not going to be me," Marina said. "At least, not with her." She recalled what Jack had said. This was the mayor's problem. And Bennett Dylan hadn't asked her.

When Kai joined them, Marina poured a glass of water for her. "You sounded great tonight."

"I love classic songs," Kai said. "And just look at Ginger out there. I want to be like her someday." She drank her water. "Now, where's that yummy tiramisu I was promised?"

"Right here," Marina said, handing her a dish. She looked over her shoulder to make sure Rhoda was gone.

"Ginger never stops," Heather said, her long ponytail swinging to the beat. After wiping down the counters, she and Cruise leaned from the serving window to watch the party.

"Now I see where you all get your energy from," Cruise said, nudging Heather.

"Ginger sets a high bar," Heather said. "We have to keep up or get run over."

"Sometimes, literally." Kai turned to Marina. "Remember when she used to make us jog on the beach? She called it Grandma Boot Camp. She even had a whistle."

"Seriously?" Cruise chuckled in disbelief.

Marina nodded. "It was tougher than it sounds. She could have been an Olympian."

"She nearly killed us all," Kai said. "But that's when she opened my eyes to performing."

"What?" Heather leaned forward with interest. "I haven't heard this story."

"She made us put on skits and sing," Kai said. "I don't know if she was entertaining us or herself and her friends."

"When was this?" Heather asked.

"During the summers we spent at Ginger's to give our folks a break," Marina replied. *Long before the accident that robbed them of their parents*, she thought, catching her sister's eye. Kai was very young then, but she understood what was left unsaid. That's why she and Kai and their middle sister Brooke were so close, even today.

"And now we're back in town for good," Kai said, raising a fist. "The next generation in Summer Beach."

"And working on the next," Marina said with a wink.

A shadow crossed Kai's face. "Sometime soon, I hope."

Marina immediately wished she hadn't mentioned that. Every month, Kai grew more concerned over her inability to conceive. Kai was nearing forty and understandably nervous.

As she watched Axe winding up the last set, Kai smiled wistfully. "It's hard to believe it's been almost a year since we married on stage at the Seashell."

"It's gone fast," Marina said, watching Kai eat her dessert. "How are you adapting to marriage?"

"Axe is just as wonderful as this tiramisu," Kai said between bites. "I still get all swoony when he sings in the shower. The biggest adjustment for me has been being off the road."

"I wondered about that." Her sister had been touring for years.

Kai took another creamy bite. "You've been married before, so it must have been easy for you."

Marina shook her head. "Stan and I weren't married long before he was called to serve in Afghanistan, so this has been new for me, too."

In the past year, she and Jack had to adapt to marriage and to each other. She loved him and Leo, as well as Scout, though that high-spirited, overgrown puppy sometimes trampled her garden.

Now in their forties, she and Jack had deeply ingrained habits to modify. Marina had never shared a TV remote with a man, and Jack was used to working at all hours of the night with the music on.

One year. Marina wondered if she and Jack should plan something special or spend it with Leo and the twins. Their track record for romantic dinners wasn't great.

The crowd applauded when Axe finished his final song of the evening. Kai hurried to join him, and they took their bows. However, no one was ready to leave. Still talking and laughing, the hosts and guests gathered around a huge fire pit.

Kai and Axe strolled back to the food truck. "Looks like everyone has moved on to liquid libations by the fire," she said, grinning.

Cruise swiped the counter with a cleaning rag. "Can we take off soon?"

"It's been a long day," Marina said. "You and Heather can take the truck back to the cafe. Go get some rest."

"Or not," Cruise said, exchanging an amused look with Heather.

"Whoa, I saw that," Kai said, twirling her finger at them. "What are you two up to?"

"There's a party at a friend's house in town," Heather said. "We're going to check it out."

"You'll be careful?" Marina asked out of habit.

Cruise nodded. "I'm the designated driver."

"The responsible older man," Heather said, giggling. She flicked his slightly shaggy hair. "Are those blond streaks or gray hairs?"

"Hey, I'm not that much older," Cruise said.

In fact, Cruise was probably about Blake's age, Marina realized. She remembered how a few years could make a difference at Heather's age. Her daughter had just turned twenty-one. Technically, she was an adult. Still, Marina appreciated Cruise looking out for her. Working together, they had developed a nice friendship.

She wouldn't worry tonight.

Just then, Ginger returned with her silver-haired dance partner. "Thank you, Oliver. You dance so well. That was indeed a treat."

Oliver executed a swift bow and kissed Ginger's hand.

"It was my honor and privilege, dear Ginger. I've been thinking—would you do me the honor of attending the centennial celebration with me?"

Ginger smiled demurely. "How thoughtful of you. But I wouldn't want to take you off the market, Oliver. Too many other women have their hearts set on dancing with you. How could I disappoint them?"

Kai grinned. After Oliver left, she said, "They don't make them like that anymore. His honor and privilege? Wow. May I steal that line for a show?"

"It's all yours," Ginger said, lifting her chin. "Might do your generation good to hear that."

"Sadly, we'd probably have to deliver it as comedy," Kai said. "And what a magnanimous way to decline a date." She winked at her grandmother. "Are you ready to go?"

Ginger looked wistfully at her friends chatting by the fire. "We used to dance until sunrise here on the beach. I don't think any of us will make it quite that long tonight."

"No, but those two might," Kai said, inclining her head toward Heather and Cruise.

Someone had turned on music, and Ginger swayed to another tune. "Why, I remember dancing to this at the Diplomat's Ball in Paris. I wore the most magnificent gold satin gown that was perfect with my hair. Bertrand wore a gold brocade vest to match. He was so handsome he took my breath away. And oh, my…the diplomatic intrigue at that ball changed the course of history, I'll have you know." She paused, catching her breath. "You're only young once. But you can be young forever in your mind."

Marina put her arms around Ginger's shoulder, concerned that she might be overdoing it. "You have the best memories. We love hearing them. Would you tell me more over a cup of tea tonight?"

Ginger held up a finger. "I have a better idea. Why, we could talk all night like we used to. With Jack away, you don't have to go home, do you?"

Marina shook her head. "I'd love to stay with you." She still had old clothes hanging in her former room at Ginger's.

Kai turned to Marina. "I have a feeling this party is just getting started."

Sweeping his arm around Kai, Axe said, "Why don't you join them, sweetheart? I have that construction job to finish early in the morning, so I need to turn in soon."

"You're sure you don't mind?" Kai asked.

"Go have fun," Axe replied, kissing her. "I know where you are if I need you."

"Then it's settled," Ginger said. "We'll have a slumber party. What a shame Brooke won't be there."

The three women got into Ginger's car, and Marina drove. She took the beach route home to Ginger's house, the Coral Cottage. For decades, the old beach house had sported a vivid shade of coral easily seen from the sea.

Marina's life had changed, but this house held so many memories for her and her sisters. Their grandmother had managed to both anchor their lives and give them flight. Ginger Delavie was a rare woman full of surprises.

Tonight would be no different, Marina suspected, wondering what her grandmother was up to.

3

"*W*hat a beautiful evening," Ginger said as she, Marina, and Kai approached the old beach house she had christened the Coral Cottage decades ago. "At one time, I could have danced all night."

Marina put her arm protectively around her grandmother. "You almost did."

"Dance through life when you can, my dears." Ginger opened her purse.

"I'll remember that," Marina said, laughing.

"Now, where are my keys?" Ginger made a clicking sound with her tongue.

Kai opened her spangled bag. "Hang on, I have mine handy."

While Marina waited, she paused to admire the full, plump moon and its rippling reflection over the breaking waves. The constant flow of waves provided a soothing soundtrack, transporting Marina to lazy childhood summers.

Standing on the front porch, another memory flashed

through her mind—that of landing here on a similar night after a long drive from San Francisco.

Tonight couldn't be more dissimilar. Then, her heart and pride had been decimated from losing her anchor job and fiancé on the same day due to a snide remark a colleague made on air. Admittedly, she could have handled that more professionally, but her heart was involved.

All that was in the past now. What a difference a day could make, Marina thought. If not for what she'd thought was a tragedy, she might have never met Jack or had the new life she loved today.

"Got them," Kai said, jingling her keys. She opened the door.

Marina stepped inside behind her grandmother, grateful for her presence in her life. Grandmother Ginger, who became simply Ginger when Marina couldn't pronounce the entire mouthful as a child, was the constant in her life.

"Oh, what a fabulous party," Ginger said, slipping off her satin heels. "And the night is still young."

Marina smiled. Her grandmother was in a party mood. She had always enjoyed good company, intelligent conversation, and accomplished dance partners.

Ginger flicked on the lights. "Since you're both staying, why don't you girls make yourselves comfortable? I have a surprise you'll enjoy."

"That sounds more like a command than a question." Kai slid off her glittery sandals and turned to Marina.

Marina tossed her sturdy work clogs to one side as well. "We still have old pajamas and beach clothes here."

"And I have a lovely old bottle of Margaux I've been saving for such a night." Ginger winked. "Maybe two. Who'll help me open one?"

The stairway creaked behind them. "I will," Brooke said.

Ginger clasped a hand to her heart. "Brooke, dear, you gave me a fright. What in heaven's name are you doing here?"

"There's too much testosterone at my house." Brooke shuddered. "Chip invited friends over to rebuild a car, and all the boys are there. Some boxing match is on, and they were screaming at the TV and hurling insults at each other. So, I left. They won't miss me until they're hungry for breakfast."

"Did you have anything to eat?" Marina asked.

"I raided the fridge," Brooke replied. "I've been upstairs relaxing and reading books on gardening. I hardly ever have a chance to do that."

Their middle sister grew organic vegetables that she sold at the farmers market along with Marina's baked goods.

"We're having a slumber party," Kai said. "Stay with us. Since Heather has taken your room, you can stay with me in my old room."

Brooke's face lit. "That sounds like fun. I'll let Chip know." She left her Birkenstocks in the corner with the rest of the discarded shoes.

"I'm glad that's settled." Ginger brought out the vintage wine and her finest crystal glasses.

Upstairs, Marina changed out of her chef jacket, and Kai shed her fancy dress. They brushed out their hair and changed into soft cotton pajamas they'd left in their old rooms.

"Ready," Marina said as they padded down the stairs.

The four women gathered in the living room on the white canvas, slip-covered sofas strewn with bright beach pillows. Kai lit candles, and Marina turned on Ginger's favorite soft jazz music.

Brooke withdrew a cork from the vintage bottle of wine.

"This aroma is amazing. It smells rich and delicious." She poured a glass and handed it to Ginger. "See what you think."

Ginger sipped the dark, ruby-red liquid. "Oh, yes. Exquisite. It was worth waiting for."

After Brooke poured three more glasses, Ginger raised hers in a toast. "I love having all my girls together," Ginger said, raising her glass to them. "Here's to you, and here's to us. What a rare treat this is."

"With the rarest wine of wine and the rarest of women," Marina added, touching her glass to Ginger's.

"We should do this more often," Kai said. "Before I'm tied down with kiddos." She gave a wistful smile. "I hope I didn't miss my chance."

"Now, you've only just started trying," Ginger said. "And medical science can be a great help if needed."

Kai chewed her lip. "You all began much earlier than me. Getting pregnant is easier when you're young."

"Not necessarily," Marina said, stroking her sister's hand. She didn't want Kai to have that mindset, although her sister might have a physiological issue, too.

Kai sat on the floor by the coffee table, folding her long legs into a cross-legged position. "I feel like I'm running out of time, so I'm considering other options. Axe and I really want a family of little thespians."

"And you will have that, my dear," Ginger said. "One way or another. What you hold in your mind, you can create, though not always as you might have initially imagined."

"You could borrow my wolf pack trio," Brooke said. "But you might never want children after spending a day with them. If I have any more, they'll be up for grabs."

Ginger rested her hand on Kai's shoulder. "Make an

appointment with a doctor. Then you'll know if you have other challenges. Axe, too."

"We've talked about that," Kai said, sipping her wine. "You know how guys are. He's a big, lovable Montana cowboy at heart. Nothing wrong with him, right?"

Ginger listened thoughtfully. "Sometimes a man needs a little prodding."

Marina could almost see the wheels spinning in Ginger's mind, and she wondered what her grandmother had in mind. The conversation shifted to Brooke and her three boys.

"At least I have more of Chip's support now," Brooke said. "Raising three boys is not for the faint of heart, but now that my husband is acting like a grown-up and not one of them—tonight excluded—our home life has improved."

"How is that?" Marina asked, clasping her knees.

"I feel like I have my husband back," Brooke confided. "And the boys are learning valuable life skills. Laundry, basic cooking, and yard work. Chip finally agreed they should know how to feed themselves as well as change the brakes on a car."

They all laughed, though Marina understood. "Preparing children for adulthood is a long process."

"And how is Jack doing with that?" Brooke asked.

"I'm including Jack in that," Marina said, grinning. "Sometimes I don't know who to admonish first—Jack, Leo, or Scout. At least Jack tries to be responsible, and Leo's mother is wonderful. Vanessa and I are becoming good friends. As for Scout, well, I'm resigned to the fact that dog provides our comic relief."

"To Scout," Kai said. "We all need a good laugh."

Everyone raised their glass in a toast to Scout.

Ginger smiled. "Learning to live with what we can't

change is the secret to wisdom. And laughter is one key to longevity."

"But change is often what we need," Marina said, inclining her head. "After the twins left for university, it was hard being alone. That's probably why I was susceptible to Grady's attention."

"And because of that, you took your time with Jack," Ginger said. "A wise decision."

"It's still an adjustment," Marina said. "I'm around people all day at the cafe, and when I come home, I often walk into a den of chaos, too."

"Do you have any time for yourself?" Brooke asked. "That's why I started gardening. I'm there, but out of the house. It helps."

"I try to walk on the beach," Marina replied. "Someday, I'd like to build an observation deck on the roof so we can look out to sea, watch the sunset, and relax after Leo goes to sleep. Maybe we'll do that for our anniversary celebration."

"That's coming up soon for both of us," Kai said. "We've planned a romantic weekend in Temecula. Wine, hiking, and hot air balloons—what's not to love?"

"Maybe we'll do something after the busy summer season." Marina wondered if she and Jack might do something like that. She would bring it up with him.

But their anniversary was also the weekend of the Summer Beach Centennial Celebration, and Leo had his heart set on going with his father and his friend Samantha. This was a big event in town for everyone.

They continued talking and laughing. After a while, Marina stifled a yawn. She glanced at the clock. It was growing late, and Heather was still out.

Ginger followed her line of sight. "Are you concerned about your daughter?"

"A little," Marina replied. "Does she often stay out this late?"

"Not with her busy schedule," Ginger said.

"She's with Cruise," Kai said, shrugging. "What's there to worry about?"

Brooke threw Kai a look. "Everything. You have a lot to learn about being a parent, but by the third kid, you won't stress nearly as much. That's why my youngest is barely housebroken."

"I doubt if I'll have the biological clock time for three," Kai said. "Unless I produce twins like Marina."

"Remember, I had two first-borns," Marina said pointedly. "That's a challenge in itself." She ran a finger around the rim of her wine glass, enjoying this banter with her sisters.

"Double the stress," Brooke said. "Especially because you were on your own."

"Ginger saw me through it, though." Marina put her arm around her grandmother. She was still thinking about Heather.

"Don't worry, dear," Ginger said softly. "She is a smart young woman."

"I'm trying not to." Yet, Marina suspected Heather wasn't telling her everything, even though her daughter was an adult and had a right to her privacy.

At least, that's what the logical part of Marina's brain believed.

Marina told them about Blake, the kind vet they'd met on the beach. "Heather seemed interested, but I don't know if she's heard from him. I've been hoping Blake would call or visit."

Kai swirled her wine. "Because you're concerned about that tattooed cook, right? He's awfully cute."

"Cruise is talented, but I don't think he's boyfriend mate-rial. At least for Heather." Marina touched Kai's hand. "She has always looked up to you. Has she confided anything about who she's interested in?"

Kai inclined her head. "No, but you guys talk, don't you?"

"Usually." Although maybe she wasn't anymore. "I'm always there for her, even if we're not under the same roof now."

"She knows that." Kai raised her brow. "Are you saying you're worried that Heather and Ethan might feel neglected since you spend more time with Jack and Leo?"

Marina considered that. "The twins like Jack, and they're always welcome at the house. Besides, they have their own lives now. Isn't that the goal?"

Ginger nodded thoughtfully.

Ethan shared an apartment with a friend in San Diego. With his mind set on golf, he was living the life of his dreams now.

Marina and Jack had offered Heather their guest room, but she preferred staying at the Coral Cottage with Ginger. That worked for all of them, and Marina didn't worry about Ginger being alone.

Still, she was anxious about Heather. She would have a talk with her soon.

Brooke rearranged the pillows behind her back and stretched out. "Have you heard about the farmers market float Cookie has organized for the centennial parade?"

Kai's eyes lit with interest. "I haven't seen it, but I think they're working on it in someone's barn. Do you know whose?"

"Marilyn and Bob, that couple who sell organic herbs and fruit at the market," Brooke replied. "They host fabulous parties on their ranch. Cookie has been very hush-hush about it, so I imagine it will be spectacular. Everything Marilyn touches turns out gorgeous."

"And I've heard the Java Beach float will be quite a contender as well," Ginger added. "Mitch is working on a vintage beach float. However, I think he's outgrowing his workshop."

"Is there a contest for the best float?" Marina asked.

"That's the rumor," Brooke said.

The conversation swiftly changed to plans for the centennial celebration. With everything going on in her life, Marina hadn't been keeping up with all the celebration events, so her sisters quickly filled her in about different groups that planned to participate. No wonder Rhoda was desperate for help. "A parade of floats is a big undertaking."

"All the way down Main Street." Kai laughed. "But these aren't high-tech, New York-style floats. I ran into Jen at Nailed It, and she told me that people are building scenes on trailers they can tow behind pickup trucks. Still, the work going into those sounds extravagant for Summer Beach."

"A neighboring community had a parade a few years ago before you girls returned," Ginger explained. "So the bar has been set quite high. Everyone in town will be there. And a lot of visitors."

"Where are people building these?" Marina asked.

"Wherever they can," Ginger replied. "In their garages, I imagine."

"But not everyone has a garage." Marina wasn't involved, but she had an idea. "Carol and Hal have a ware-house—the old fruit-packing facility they use for recording and filming. Maybe they'd let people work in there in case it rains. They often come to the cafe, so I could ask them."

"Brilliant idea," Ginger said, looking at her with admiration.

"I think the whole event is so exciting." Kai's eyes widened with excitement. "Our neighbors are decorating golf carts and children's bikes. Axe and I will perform songs to preview our upcoming musical. The only hitch in this whole event is Rhoda. The word is she split."

"She had some family issues." Marina sighed at the mention of that woman's name.

Kai shrugged. "I suppose people can just line up, cruise Main Street, and call it a parade."

"There's a lot more to it than that," Marina said, surprised at Kai's cavalier solution. "Someone will have to direct the flow and look out for bottlenecks. Participants will be waving at friends in the crowd, and possibly not paying attention to where they're going. Why, children on bikes could get run over by floats or cars. It could be quite dangerous."

"Exactly," Kai said, slicing the air with her hand. "See? You understand these things. I hadn't even thought about that."

A quick look passed between Kai, Ginger, and Brooke. "Oh, no," Marina said, holding up her palms. "I'm not volunteering."

"You do have some good ideas," Ginger mused, swirling the wine in her glass. A smile curved her lips.

Brooke nodded enthusiastically. "Marina, you're a good organizer. Besides the cafe, remember the Taste of Summer Beach event?"

Suddenly, Marina felt a tingling sensation on her neck, as if she'd just stumbled right into some sort of plan. "Really, I don't think I could do it justice."

"At least think about it," Kai said, lobbing a pillow at her.

"Hey," Marina said, dodging the pillow while holding her wine glass high. "If you waste this Margaux, you'll have to answer to Ginger. And replace the slipcovers."

While the others laughed and talked, Marina sipped her wine, considering the problem facing Summer Beach. Should she take on the project? Organizing the community for such a festive, happy event could be fun, but the centennial also landed on her first anniversary. That would be asking a lot of Jack.

If he even remembered, that is. So far, he hadn't mentioned it at all.

4

*J*ack hesitated beside an outdoor table at an upscale cafe in busy Santa Monica near the beach. Mildly surprised, he glanced around. Was this really the place Chaz had chosen? It was so exposed.

Scout leaned against his leg as if he sensed they were in the wrong place.

After a moment, Jack pulled out a wrought iron chair under a mustard-yellow umbrella and sat down. "Down, boy."

Scout flopped onto Jack's sneakers, panting.

Behind him, a cheerful voice chirped, "What can I get you today?"

He looked up at a young woman who stepped into view. "Actually, I'm expecting someone. But I might not be in the right place."

"Is that your party?" she asked, stepping to one side.

A man with perfectly styled steel-gray hair lifted his chin

to Jack. He could pass for a model for a men's health magazine cover.

Chaz. He'd gone gray since Jack had seen him, but he was still immaculately dressed. How long had it been since he'd seen him? Almost a decade. That was during the trial Jack had covered.

The older man joined him. "You're as punctual as ever, Jack."

Chaz still had his New England boarding school accent. "So are you. Thanks for meeting me."

"What are you wearing?" Chaz lifted an eyebrow in mild disdain.

"A fishing vest," Jack said, tugging his baseball cap lower over his forehead. He felt a twinge of guilt about what he'd told Marina, but he didn't want to worry her.

"You were always a little wrinkled in the courtroom." Chaz brushed a small piece of lint from his impeccable hand-finished jacket that must have been in storage for years. "I would have preferred to meet at the Los Angeles Country Club, but my membership appears to have lapsed while I was away. Just as well, I suppose. I could not have taken you there dressed like that. Or with that creature glued to your feet."

Jack suppressed a smile. By *away*, Chaz meant in prison. He had once been a money manager to the elite. He worked for his father-in-law, whom Jack had helped put away by exposing his financial schemes.

During his incarceration, Chaz had spearheaded budgeting and investing workshops for inmates and gained early release for good behavior.

"This is your sidekick?" Chaz stretched a manicured hand to Scout, who shied away from him. "He has a limp like me."

"He was hit by a car before I adopted him." Jack laced his hands on the table. "You said you have information for me?"

"Let's eat first. Why rush?" He nodded toward a server and lifted two fingers.

Jack shifted. "I don't have a lot of time."

"What else is there? My social schedule isn't what it used to be," Chaz said. "No one was waiting for me when I returned. No job, family, or friends of any consequence. Thanks to you."

Jack held his tongue. Funny how people blamed others when they got caught. Still, Jack had also uncovered information that lessened Chaz's sentence. In appreciation, Chaz had become a source for Jack. Perhaps because he didn't have anyone else.

"You're smart," Jack said. "You can build up again. And friends who are only there when you're loaded aren't your true friends."

"What a colloquial term." Chaz gave him a bemused smile. "In my former circle, what you call friendships are based on mutual benefit. Old money is all about making new money to add to the pot. However, in my case, even the best people proved fickle. Which is why I am free to visit with you today."

A server appeared with two chilled glasses that held cocktails the color of a summer sunset and garnished with oranges. She placed them on the table.

"What's this?" Jack asked.

"An Aperol spritz," Chaz replied. "A taste of Italy, and very refreshing in the summer. The escargot is also quite good here, by the way."

Jack could play along. "One of my favorites." He could choke down a couple of snails as long as they were swimming in rivers of garlic butter.

When the server left, Jack asked, "What's so important that you wanted to meet after all these years?"

Chaz sighed. "Always straight to the point. I heard you have been asking questions. I am acquainted with a man... let's call him Jersey. Mr. Jersey, out of respect."

Jack raised an eyebrow. "Would I know him?"

"Doubtful. He has an associate. He deals in quite sophisticated financial circles. Some new strategies, some old."

"Bitcoin?" Jack ventured. "Insider trading?"

"More interesting than that." Chaz withdrew a small, ivory notecard from the interior pocket of his jacket and slid it across the table.

Jack looked at it and quickly put it back down. His pulse quickened, sensing the gravity. "Why tell me about him?"

"Perhaps I'm pursuing redemption."

"Or payback."

Chaz shook his head as if disappointed by the question. "Where are your manners?"

Scout nudged closer to Jack's leg as if to protect him. *Is Chaz playing me, or is this genuine?*

Chaz's smirk faded. "He's big news, Jack. You haven't had a good story in a while."

"You're following my career now?"

"I found myself with a great deal of time on my hands, so to speak."

"Seriously, why now?"

Chaz scrutinized him. "I'm serious about redemption. For my family's sake."

"Are you ill?" Old background information floated to mind, and Jack recalled that Chaz's mother had been quite devout. While she had since passed away, she had attended the trial, always wearing somber black, a head covering, and holding her prayer book. Maybe he was looking for an entry ticket to the pearly gates.

"No one lives forever, so we should live well while we're here," Chaz said thoughtfully. "But others don't deserve that."

Now they were getting somewhere, Jack thought, leaning forward. "What others?"

"Those who take advantage of widows and orphans or drain the life savings of hard workers."

Jack narrowed his eyes. "Redemption, huh?"

"For both of us." Chaz waved a hand.

"I have a clean conscience." Jack could say that and mean it.

Except for Leo, a situation that had been set straight now, and a couple of *faux pas* with Marina, Jack was good. Unless there were more like Leo from his past.

But no, he was sure there weren't. He had been careful; he might not have been a suitable long-term boyfriend while chasing stories around the globe, but he wasn't a one-night-stand kind of guy. Except with Vanessa.

He could admit his frailty now, although it wouldn't happen again. Not with Marina in his life.

Chaz shrugged. "Maybe there are things you've forgotten."

Jack glared at him. "I seriously doubt it," he said, taking the offensive. "And if information is manufactured about me—"

"Don't get excited." As Chaz held up his palm, an engraved gold cufflink winked in the sunlight at the edge of his slightly frayed bespoke shirt. That's not at all what I meant." He drew out a sigh. "Let's say I have a special interest."

"Do you want to tell me about that?"

Chaz gave him a tight smile. "No, I do not." Again, he reached into his pocket and withdrew a card for Jack. "Could be another Pulitzer in your future."

Jack stared at it. "What is this?"

"A breadcrumb. I trust you'll follow it and find a new set of culprits. You have quite the knack for that, I'm sorry to say."

Jack felt a sudden chill at his words, but just then, the server appeared and placed two hot dishes of escargot on the table.

Wincing, Jack glared at the steaming dish. He couldn't sit here and trade small talk with a man so criminally urbane he made his skin crawl. Or force down an equally distasteful dish. He hadn't yearned for a cigarette in months, but Chaz brought out the old desire in him again.

Biting his lip against the craving, Jack leaned forward. "While I appreciate this lead, I have to go. Let me know if you come up with anything else."

"Trust me, that will be quite enough. What a shame you must leave just as the escargot arrived. Are the fish on a schedule?"

Jack ignored the dig. "More for you, Chaz."

He stood and strode from the table, with Scout trotting beside him. He cut through the patio and saw their server at a wait stand. He pulled a credit card from his pocket. "Would you put the bill on this, please?"

"Sure," she replied. As the server rang it up, Jack looked back at Chaz. "I have to go. Know anyone who'd like to join him?"

She smiled. "Wish I did. He always seems lonely. It's a shame, given he was so successful back then. Poor guy. Have you seen any of his films?"

Jack almost felt sorry for him, too. For now, he'd play

along with whatever story Chaz was telling people. "Every one of them," he said.

Having completed what he set out to do in Santa Monica, Jack drove back to Summer Beach. He had wanted to surprise Marina, but she had called to say she was staying at Ginger's house with her sisters. She sounded so giddy and happy that he decided to let her have her fun. Besides, he needed a good night's sleep.

If he could rest after that creepy encounter with Chaz.

The next morning, a text pinged his phone. It was Vanessa, Leo's mother. Jack swung his legs over the edge of the bed and rubbed his face.

He tapped back. *Is Leo okay?*

Yes, but he wants you to pick him up earlier. Is that possible?

Jack would do anything for Leo. *Half an hour?*

Vanessa agreed. Next, he called Marina, who still sounded sleepy. "How was your slumber party?"

"Fun, but painful this morning. How was the fishing?"

"The catch didn't look very good, so I came home early. I missed you." He loved hearing her voice early in the morning before the demands of the day stole their attention. They talked for a few minutes. She wouldn't be home until later, so he promised to stop by the cafe.

Jack showered and dressed, leaving his hair damp. As he stretched a T-shirt over his shoulders, he thought about what Chaz had said.

Maybe he was slightly wrinkled, but he was happy this way.

He'd taken this assignment to put money aside for Leo and have a cushion for Marina. Their anniversary was also coming up. When he worked at the newspaper in New York, an assistant had helped him keep track of his calendar. He didn't want Marina to think he'd forgotten their anniversary, though he needed to confirm the date. Or check their marriage license—if he could find it.

He slid on a pair of sandals, grabbed his keys, and headed out the door. Simple beachwear was good enough in Summer Beach.

Vanessa's voice sounded through the open window. "The door is open, come in."

Jack stepped inside, feeling out of place in her home. The room was beautifully furnished with casual, overstuffed furnishings and vivid, collectible Mexican artwork she had inherited from her parents. Flowers filled vases and perfumed the air.

Vanessa always had a certain refinement about her. Jack couldn't have chosen a better mother for his son, not that he'd been aware of it at the time. *One furtive night on the eve of what might have been their last day of life…*

He and Vanessa had been friends and colleagues before she left her position as a reporter. Now they were co-parenting Leo. It had been almost two years ago that Jack learned he had a son. Since then, he'd quit his high-pressured work and vowed to make time for Leo.

Like him, Vanessa had also married. Noah was a medical researcher and held an important position. The doctor's discovery had saved Vanessa's life.

"Good morning," Vanessa said as she walked into the room. Her full floral skirt brushed her ankles. She was looking more like her old self now. Her hair had grown back, though she wore it in a stylish short cut rather than the long, wavy style she once had. She was still more slender than she had been, but thankfully, the gaunt look of illness had passed.

Most of all, a zest for life sparkled in her eyes again. She wore bright pink lipstick that matched her blouse and the happy flush on her cheeks.

"Leo is packing his bag," she said. "I need to meet Noah at the airport, and Leo wanted to see you sooner. I hope you don't mind."

"Never. I'm always there for Leo."

Vanessa gestured to an overstuffed chair in the living room. "May I get you anything to drink?"

"No, I'm fine, thanks." He eased onto the chair. "I'm working on a story again," he added, venturing into professional territory they had once shared.

"You are?"

"You sound surprised."

Vanessa furrowed her brow. "You covered some rough assignments. I know you find that satisfying, but is that wise now with your new life?"

"You're concerned for Leo's sake." Jack had already thought of that. "Don't be. I'm not investigating life-threatening stories. No wars, no government overthrows, no foreign travels, no whizzing bullets. White collar stories only."

Vanessa arched an eyebrow and considered that. "Dangerous situations can develop when money is at stake. You know that as well as I do."

Jack shifted uneasily in the chair. "There's always a risk. But what do you want me to do, Vanessa? I enjoy illustrating for Ginger's books, but we both know I'm trained for more than that. My mission is to make a difference. And I need to put funds aside for Leo's education."

"You don't have to do that," Vanessa said.

"Of course, I do," Jack said, bristling. "I'm his father, and I'm way behind in my job, thanks to your decision."

Vanessa raised her brow. "I meant to say that my parents made financial arrangements for Leo's education in their wills. He will have access to whatever he needs. I know I told you that."

"You did." Although that should have been a relief, Jack still scowled. "I'm not shirking my duty. I'm his father, and I have accepted that responsibility. I will provide for his education."

"I didn't mean to intimate that you wouldn't." Vanessa gave him a long look. "I understand how that might hurt your pride. But remember, I never wanted anything from you. If I hadn't been so gravely ill, I never would have reached out to you." She held up a hand before Jack could protest. "I realize that was a mistake, too."

Jack had turned this over in his mind many times. He'd forgiven Vanessa for that decision, yet it didn't bring back the lost years with Leo. His son's first steps, his first day in school, his first everything—Jack had missed so much.

Still, he had to ask the hard question. "Now that you're in remission, do you regret having contacted me?"

A small sigh escaped Vanessa's lips. "It was the right thing to do. If I had died, he would have needed you. I always knew you would be there for him if I asked."

Jack looked down at his hands. "So, you're saying that if you hadn't been ill, I never would have known about him?"

Vanessa flicked a glance at her watch. "Jack, we've been over this."

She was right. However, the closer he got to Leo, the more he resented Vanessa's concealment. Because now he knew the joy he'd been robbed of.

"I'll admit, discovering that I had a ten-year-old son was a shock. It took some getting used to. But now, I want to be a real father to him. Not just the back-up plan. He'll be twelve soon, and before we know it, he'll go away for his university education."

Vanessa was quiet for a moment. "I see your point. It was selfish of me to keep him to myself. You understand the reason I did that."

"Of course." Jack nodded. That was seared in his mind. "Your parents wouldn't have accepted me, and you didn't want to marry. But now, here you are, married after all."

"I didn't realize I could fall so deeply in love." Vanessa smiled. "Nothing against you, of course. We were colleagues and friends. And now, I hope we can remain friends and co-parents."

Leo raced into the room. "Dad, you came." He flung his arms around Jack's neck.

"I'm always here for you, son."

"I'll get my bag," Leo said, racing back to his room.

Vanessa placed a hand on his arm. "Be careful. Leo needs you now."

Jack choked back a reply and nodded. He still needed to work on his parenting skills, but he was determined to be a better father. And a better husband. The question was, how would he reconcile those desires with the risks of his work?

5

"*Two* orders of fish tacos for my best customers," Marina said, placing a pair of coral plates on the rustic dining table in the open-air kitchen. Jack and Leo eyed the food hungrily.

Each plate held artfully arranged tacos stuffed with grilled mahi mahi, crisp cabbage, shredded lettuce, and sliced avocado with a drizzle of her special sauce.

"Yum," Leo said, bouncing on the bench.

Jack caught her hand. "I sure appreciate this, sweetheart."

"It's what I do." Marina bent for a quick kiss. "And why wouldn't I feed two of my favorite men?" Along with Ethan, of course. "You should come more often."

"When I'm working, I hardly even think about it," Jack said. "There's usually something in the fridge."

"I make sure of that. You need fuel after those morning runs with the mayor." Over the past year, they had worked out their respective routines. While her schedule at the cafe was more predictable than Jack's, he had to care for Leo, too.

During the summer, Jack often brought Leo by for lunch, just as he had when they were dating. When Leo was with his mother, Jack often worked through lunch.

But lately, Marina sensed something was weighing on Jack's mind. He hadn't talked much about the story he was writing. Whether that was his usual way of working or he felt he couldn't confide in her, Marina didn't know. She didn't want to appear nosy, and she respected the confidentiality he gave his sources. Still, he seemed preoccupied.

Jack bit into the taco and quickly took a drink. "That's spicy today. Too much for you, Leo?"

"Yeah, but they're good. Don't let Scout have any." Leo grinned at Marina.

She caught the look, recalling when Scout had bounded into a restaurant in agony after he'd eaten one of Jack's tacos. Still, patrons preferred to adjust the heat level in their dishes.

Marina turned to her cook. "Cruise, did you do something different with the seasoning?"

The younger man flushed. "Just something new I whipped up." He handed her a chunk of fish that had just come off the fire. "What do you think?"

Marina took the piece. "It's good, but it's spicier than customers expect, so we'd have to note that on the menu. Customers want their favorite dishes to taste the same. Let me know before you do that again."

She turned to Jack. "Do you and Leo want me to replace those tacos with something milder?"

Leo shook his head. "This is good," Jack said, draining his water glass.

"I can tell." She didn't want to make a scene in front of

Leo and Jack, but this wasn't the first time Cruise had changed the recipe without her knowledge. Several dishes had been returned to the kitchen because of his edits.

She filled a pitcher of water and placed it on the table for Jack and Leo. "You'll need this."

Heather whisked into the kitchen. "Hey, Mom. I have a request for extra avocados and sauce for the tacos on table four. They said they know you."

Marina leaned over the counter and waved in acknowledgment. She had plenty of regular customers now. "No charge on those extras."

Just then, a tall, good-looking man she didn't recognize walked in. He had sandy blond hair and broad shoulders. Yet, there was something familiar about him.

Then she remembered.

"Heather, is that Blake? The aquatic veterinarian we met at the beach."

Her daughter's lips parted, and she whipped around. "Sure is."

"Is anyone with him?"

"I don't think so."

"Tell him to join us at the chef's table. He shouldn't have to eat alone."

Leo looked up. His cute face was smeared with sauce. "The guy who rescued the sea lions?"

Marina tossed another napkin to Jack, and he wiped Leo's face in one broad swoop.

"I got this, Dad." Leo looked a little embarrassed.

"I know you do. Just giving you a hand." Jack mussed Leo's hair.

Marina smiled at the exchange. Leo was still a messy little boy, but he was becoming more aware. That was all part of growing up, she recalled. With her twins practically on their own, she enjoyed having Leo around. He lessened her empty nest feeling.

Jack wasn't interested in starting a family because he had Leo. That was fine with Marina. The thought of having more children was daunting. Between Jack, Leo, and the cafe, she had plenty to keep her busy.

Heather and Ethan were busy living their lives, though she still provided emotional support. Her life was as full as she wanted, and she loved the progress they were making toward becoming a blended family. She hadn't realized she could love someone as much as she had once loved Stan.

As she poured extra sauce onto a dish and arranged sliced avocados, she glanced at her handsome husband, who looked slightly wrinkled today with his hair in disarray. She smiled to herself; she and Jack were perfectly imperfect for each other.

Marina put the dishes on a tray for Heather. "Here you are." She looked up, caught Blake's eye, and waved to him.

"I'll be back with our sea lion savior." Heather picked up the order and sailed from the kitchen.

Moments later, she returned, guiding Blake into the kitchen area. Marina's intuition hummed, and she noticed that Heather's cheeks were flushed with a tinge of pink. Perhaps Blake was here for more than just the food.

Cruise turned around, noticing that, too.

"How's that order, Cruise?" Marina asked.

"Coming right out." The younger man went back to work.

Blake grinned when he saw them all. "I had business nearby, so I thought I'd stop by for lunch. It's good to see you all again."

"We're glad you came," Marina said, watching Heather's reaction. She seemed a little nervous.

Blake glanced around the kitchen. "So this is your natural habitat. Very nice."

"Good to see you," Jack said. "Have a seat at the family table. You never know who will drop in. You said you've been here before?"

"I met friends here a few months ago." Blake settled at the table and turned to Heather. "What's good today?"

Heather gestured to a chalkboard with the daily specials. "Fish tacos, shrimp salad, seafood pizza. We also have turkey sliders and sweet potato fries." She pulled a printed menu from a menu holder. "And anything you see there."

"The fish tacos look good. I'll have those."

"They're a little spicy today," Marina warned with a glance at Cruise.

Blake grinned. "Even better."

"Okay, good choice," Heather said. "How is the family of sea lions?"

As Heather poured a glass of water for him, he smiled, watching her movements. "We've been nursing the little guy back to health. We plan to release them soon. Since you were the ones who found them, would you like to be there for their release?"

"That would be amazing," Heather said. "When?"

"I'll check and let you know. Should be in a few days."

"I'd really like that." Heather blushed again. "I'd better check on my tables."

Leo turned his face to Jack. "Can we go, too?"

"We'll see," Jack replied. "Your mother has those summer day camps planned for you."

"Oh, yeah." Leo looked disappointed.

Blake leaned toward Leo. "If you can't make it, I'll take a video for you. And you can visit some other time."

"Okay. Cool." That satisfied Leo, and he went back to wolfing down his tacos.

Cruise slid the grilled fish onto a platter and passed it to Marina to finish. While she worked, Jack asked Blake about his visit.

"I met with a group of people interested in funding more marine research and rescue here in Summer Beach," Blake said. "They've made me an offer to head up the effort."

Jack asked, "Does that mean you're moving here?"

"I haven't accepted the position yet," Blake said. "But I'm seriously considering it."

Heather returned and listened to the conversation. The lunch rush was over, though some people lingered, enjoying the sunshine.

Blake wasn't much older than Heather, and they were clearly drawn to each other. Marina liked him, or what she saw of him so far. She glanced at Jack, and they traded a small smile.

Marina wiped her hands on a towel. "Heather, we're not that busy anymore. Why don't you take a break and talk to Blake while I clean up?"

Heather grinned and tucked a stray hair behind her ear. "Could I have a taco, Mom?"

"Sure." Cruise had another piece of fish coming off the grill, and Marina prepared a dish for her. "Here you go. Sit down and relax. You've had a busy day."

Marina glanced at the tables, which were emptying now. This was the time of day she enjoyed, after a successful, busy lunch run when she could sit down and chat with Jack and Leo, or other customers. Sometimes, Ginger or other friends joined her in the kitchen at the chef's table.

Heather and Blake were talking with ease about their

studies and plans for the future. Heather spoke about her major in marketing, her voice tinged with uncertainty. "I have another year left, but I'm still figuring out where I want it to take me."

Blake leaned forward, looking intrigued. "Marketing is versatile. You could do that anywhere. My work is by sea, but I wouldn't have it any other way."

"If I can, I'd like to stay here." Heather grinned. "I love Summer Beach. And being around my family—old and new." She put her arm around Leo. "It's cool having a new brother."

Leo beamed at her, and when Blake looked puzzled, Marina explained. "Jack and I married last year. My grandmother lives in that cottage over there."

"Have you lived here a long time?" Blake asked.

"Off and on," Marina replied. "I worked in San Francisco for years and returned a couple of years ago. Heather grew up in the city."

"And I moved from New York," Jack added. "Never thought I'd end up here, but it's a great place. Especially for kids."

"I can see that." Blake looked thoughtful. "There's a lot I could do here."

Marina could practically feel the unspoken words.

Blake asked more about Summer Beach, and he told them about how he'd recently graduated from the university in San Diego, though he'd volunteered in marine rescue for years.

After they ate, Blake glanced at his watch. "I should head back. But I'll call you about the release."

"I'll be there, for sure," Heather said.

Despite his words, Blake hesitated, seemingly reluctant to leave. "I have a book in my car about sea lions. It's one I often give to kids when I speak at schools. Maybe Leo would like it?"

"Cool," Leo said, his face brightening.

Blake touched Heather's hand. "Want to walk with me to my car?"

"I'll be right back with it," Heather said to Leo.

As the two walked away, Cruise watched after them, then threw down his towel. He'd been cleaning up and not saying much while they were here. "Mind if I take off now?"

"Go ahead," Marina said. "See you tomorrow."

"Can I go play with Scout, Dad?"

"Just keep him out of Ginger's garden," Jack replied. "We don't want to replant it again." He turned to Marina and took her hand, folding it between his. Nodding toward the garden, he said, "Remember that day? That was quite the meet-cute."

Marina laughed at the old writer's term. "That wasn't our very first meeting, but in hindsight, it was kind of cute." She glanced at Heather and Blake. "So was that."

Jack studied her. "What do you think about Blake?"

"He seems kind, smart, and accomplished." Everything a mother could want for her daughter, though she didn't want to push her. "Heather is still young. She has plenty of time."

Jack nodded. "She and Cruise seem pretty friendly, too. But that's her prerogative." He paused. "How old did you say you were when you met Stan?"

Marina pressed her lips together and sighed. "About that age. But I had already been through a lot with my parents. I seemed older."

Chuckling, Jack pulled her closer and kissed her. "Heather is smart. Someday, she'll fall in love and start her own life. Will you be ready for that?"

"I'll have to be." And then, a shocking thought occurred to her. In a few years, she could be a grandmother. "Life rushes at us, doesn't it? I still feel young inside."

Running a finger along her cheek, he smiled. "And you are."

"But when you see your children grow up, you realize how fast time is going."

Jack studied her as he held her in his arms. "So, let's slow it down. Not by cramming more into each day, but by enjoying the time we have. How about a walk on the beach tonight with me?"

"I'd like that." A thought that had been nagging her surfaced again. "And maybe you'll tell me what's been on your mind lately."

Jack looked surprised. "It's this story I've been working on. It has layers and complications."

"Want to talk about it?"

He shook his head. "Sometimes I flounder before I find the right angle for the story."

Marina suspected there was more he wasn't telling her, and she wondered why. Maybe he would confide in her this evening.

After a light supper, Leo left with his mother and Noah. Marina wiped down the vintage blue enamel stovetop while Jack finished washing dishes and dried his hands.

"Still up for that walk?" he asked.

Marina slid her arms around his waist. "Looks like it's a beautiful sunset. Let's go."

They strolled through the neighborhood of neat vintage bungalows toward the beach, pausing to say hello to neighbors. Some, like them, were new to the area, while others had lived in Summer Beach for years. Many on this street knew Ginger because she had taught math at the local school after Bertrand died.

When they reached the beach, the sun was dipping toward the horizon. Marina's sandals made soft imprints on the wet sand as she walked beside Jack, their fingers interlaced. The evening sun cast a golden hue over the waves, making them shimmer with a sheen of gold. This was a view Marina never tired of.

The fresh scent of the sea and the rhythm of the waves should have been calming, but a distinct unease curled in the pit of her stomach. Jack had been distant lately, and she wondered if he was always like this when he worked on a story.

"You've been working awfully late at night," Marina began tentatively.

"Ginger's publisher needs my new illustrations."

"That's not what I mean." She tried again. "Is everything okay with the new story you're working on?"

Jack hesitated for a split second, too brief for anyone who didn't know him as intimately as Marina did. "It's just a financial piece," he replied with a shrug. "Following the money, you know. Sounds more glamorous than it is, but it can be tedious and dull."

Marina frowned slightly. She'd been married to Jack long enough to recognize the way his jaw tensed and how he avoided her gaze. He was deflecting, and it set off alarms in her mind.

"If there's something more to it, you can talk to me," Marina said, squeezing his hand.

He gave a tight half-smile. "It's just numbers, honey. Nothing to worry about."

She didn't like how he was placating her, but she also

understood why journalists kept their sources confidential and guarded their stories until they were ready to release them. "Can't tell me, huh?"

"Afraid not."

"I see." Marina watched the waves racing to the shoreline.

"When I can, you'll be the first to know. I promise."

She accepted that. She had always admired Jack's tenacity and professionalism. As a former news anchor, she understood his commitment. Yet, despite understanding why he couldn't share what he was working on, she felt a cloud of unease she couldn't shake off.

"If it gets too intense, you can step back," she ventured, biting her lip.

Jack stopped, turning to face her. The sun's last rays caught his face, highlighting the lines that stress and time had etched. "Marina, this is what I do. It's who I am."

She stared at him. He hadn't addressed her statement, but she wouldn't ask again. Love and worry warred in her heart. She wanted to press, to get him to confide in her, to share the weight of whatever burden he was shouldering. But she also recognized the fierce determination in his eyes. The look that told her he was a man of unwavering principle.

The look she recognized when she looked in the mirror, too.

Marina sighed, leaning into him. "Just promise me you'll be careful. If not for me, for Leo's sake."

Jack wrapped an arm around her, pulling her close. "Always."

As they continued their walk, Marina's mind raced. She trusted Jack, but her concern lingered. Just when the summer had looked so bright.

6

*M*arina tore fresh leaves for garnish in her kitchen at the Coral Cafe, and the fresh scent of basil filled the air. She wiped her hands on a dishtowel and glanced at Cruise, who was plating a veggie omelet. He passed the plate and turned back to the stove.

Marina had barely had a chance to talk to Heather lately. Yesterday, her daughter had lingered with Blake by his car, and when she returned, she gave the book Blake promised to Leo and raced to her room. Through an open window in the cottage, Marina heard her talking excitedly on the phone with a friend.

Oh, to be that age again, she thought. Still, she had it pretty good now with Jack in her life, and she wouldn't trade that for anything.

Cruise glanced at her with a studied air of casualness. "Who was that guy Heather was talking to yesterday?"

Marina looked up. Cruise had been quiet today, but now he was a little too nonchalant. "Someone we met on our camping trip. Blake is an aquatic veterinarian."

When Cruise didn't respond, she ventured a question that had been on her mind. "After the anniversary event, did you and Heather have a good time at the other party? You were out awfully late."

Cruise shrugged. "It was okay."

Maybe Heather and Cruise were just friends, after all. She wasn't getting anything out of either one of them.

Marina thought about how lovely her daughter was, and how little Heather realized that. Why shouldn't she have a few young men interested in her?

Heather was naturally shy, although she was improving by working at the cafe. If there was one gift Marina wished she could instill in her daughter, it would be a healthy dose of self-confidence. Heather had so much more talent and potential than she realized.

Marina recalled feeling the same way when she was young. But as she'd grown older, she'd been forced to step outside her comfort zone to support the twins after Stan died. She didn't wish anything that dramatic on her daughter.

"Order up," Marina said, adding a side of chopped fruit, an extra garnish of basil, and thin, julienned green onions on the omelet.

Heather swooped into the kitchen area. "Thanks."

"Tell Gilda hello for me," Marina said. She had many of her customer's favorite orders memorized.

Heather tucked a strand of dark blond hair back into her thick ponytail. "She loves her basil and green onions."

Marina enjoyed her regulars and catered to them. She placed a few tiny morsels of bacon into a small bowl. "This is for Pixie. Have to keep that Chihuahua happy."

"Thanks, Mom." Heather scooped up the plate and

sailed toward Gilda, who sported vivid pink hair and a matching backpack for her frisky dog.

Marina glanced at the time. Her grandmother had asked her to come to the house. "I need to step away for a meeting Ginger arranged with the mayor. Will you handle the kitchen?"

"Sure, we've got this," Cruise said, casting a look in Heather's direction as something caught his eye. Distracted, he hesitated a little too long.

Marina slid a skillet off a burner. "These potatoes are getting toasty."

"Oh, sorry," Cruise said, his face flushing.

This wasn't like him. Cruise had turned out to be a better cook than she'd expected. That is, if he could keep his mind on his work.

"Watch the stove, please. Food waste adds up." This wasn't the first time she'd warned him about that, or about detouring from her recipes. Like yesterday.

Cruise quickly swung back into a rhythm. "Yes, ma'am."

"You put the raw langoustine in the refrigerator, right?"

"Um, sure," he said quickly, his gaze darting toward the refrigerator as if uncertain.

She paused. "Does that mean you did, or you didn't?"

"It's all in there."

"Wouldn't want that to spoil. It will be a popular lunch special today. You need to prepare it right away."

When she arrived this morning before the cafe opened for breakfast, she'd seen Heather eating a langoustine and eggs dish that Cruise had made for her. They'd been immersed in conversation.

Marina brushed crumbs from her floral print chef jacket. While she respected the classic white jacket, this fit her casual cafe theme. "Call me if you need anything."

She made her way outside and took a deep breath, inhaling the salty sea air as the morning sun warmed her face.

A horn tapped, and Marina turned.

"Hey, you," Kai called from her new SUV as she pulled alongside the house. Her sister stepped out in a pink sundress and glittery sandals. Giant pink-tinted, cat-eye sunglasses perched on her nose.

"Love the movie-star shades." Marina grinned. She never knew how her sister would turn up. All the world was indeed Kai's stage.

"Too much is just about right, don't you think?" Without waiting for a reply, Kai lowered the sunglasses. "Did you get summoned, too?"

"Seems so." Marina embraced her sister. "I wonder what Ginger is up to now. She wouldn't say, other than it was urgent."

"I hope it doesn't take too long," Kai said, glancing at her phone with a slight frown.

"Do you have an appointment or something?"

Kai responded with a small smile. "At the clinic."

"Are you, you know?"

"Pregnant? I wish. I can't understand why it's taking so long. It's not for a lack of trying."

Marina poked her in the ribs. "Too much info, but thanks for sharing."

Changing the subject, she looked up at the older two-story home. "Our slumber party the other night was so much fun. We should do that again."

Kai nodded. "As much as I love my cozy new home with Axe, I kind of miss the chaos of all of us living together. We didn't have much to worry about."

Marina paused by the front door. "Can't wait to see what this mystery meeting is all about."

The door swung open, and Ginger bustled out. She was dressed in crisp denim jeans and a pristine white cotton shirt. A Panama hat with a colorful silk scarf wrapped around the brim sat atop her thick silver hair. Their grandmother still exuded style and energy.

"Here are my girls," she said warmly, pulling them both in for a hug. "But you're both late," she added. "Change of plans. We'll meet the mayor at the cafe. Let's not keep him waiting."

Marina hadn't seen Bennett Dylan at the cafe. "He hasn't arrived yet."

Ginger gestured toward the parking lot, where a black SUV was pulling in. A trim man in his mid-forties got out. "There he is now. Punctual as usual. When the mayor told me he was too busy for lunch today, I suggested we combine our meeting. That's why I changed our venue."

"What does Bennett want?" Kai asked.

Ginger shook her head. "He didn't go into detail, other than to say it has to do with the upcoming centennial celebration."

Marina's thoughts leapt ahead, her mind spinning over what the mayor might want to discuss. She already planned to bring her food truck to the event.

"Let's see what the day has in store for us," Ginger said.

Marina grinned at that. Ginger approached each day as if it held a marvelous surprise. Maybe that was her grandmother's secret.

Marina hurried back to the cafe with Ginger and Kai. On the patio, bright coral umbrellas shielded diners from the sun. Potted palm trees stood around the perimeter, and strings of lights were woven overhead, ready to illuminate the space once evening fell.

Breakfast customers still lingered at tables over coffee. The air rang with relaxed conversation and occasional laughter.

Bennett met them at the entry. "Wonderful to see you, Ginger. Thank you for meeting me today."

"You've been so busy, we've hardly seen you," Ginger said, offering her hand.

With admiration in his eyes, Bennett clasped her hand. "The centennial event planning is quite time-consuming."

They sat down, and Marina glanced toward the kitchen, where she could see Cruise. He seemed to be doing fine. On the patio, Heather was refilling water glasses and delivering meals. With her hair falling from her ponytail and her actions a little jerky, she seemed harried.

Cruise motioned to Heather, and she rushed to the kitchen.

Marina frowned, wondering what was wrong. Heather looked slightly pale, though she had seemed fine this morning when she was chatting with Cruise. Marina would talk to her after the meeting.

"Let's order right away." Marina lifted her hand to Heather, who joined them at the table.

"Cruise just told me about a special today," Heather said. "Chef's surprise."

"The special is a grilled langoustine salad," Marina said.

"Excellent," Bennett added. "And plenty of coffee."

Marina looked at Ginger and Kai, who also nodded.

While Heather served coffee, Bennett began to talk about the city's plans. Glancing around the table, he said, "Ginger, I'm here to ask you, on behalf of the entire city of Summer Beach, if you would do us the honor of serving as

Grand Marshal in the centennial parade. You have been a mainstay of Summer Beach for many years, contributing your time and knowledge toward improving our community and residents. If you need time to think about it—"

"Why waste time?" Ginger said with a perfunctory nod. "I'd be delighted."

"That's what I hoped you'd say." Bennett outlined the ceremonial duties.

As the conversation continued with parade planning, Marina's gaze drifted back to Cruise. With his sun-bleached hair falling across his forehead, he was focused now. Though with his tattoos, black jeans, and T-shirt under a stained apron, he was dressed more for clubbing than the kitchen and the budding gourmet chef he was.

Marina wondered what he was up to, but she turned her attention back to the conversation. Ginger and Bennett were brainstorming ideas.

"Many people are building floats," Bennett said. "But we lack a sense of cohesion and leadership. I hoped you and your family might help with that."

"In light of the centennial celebration, a parade should highlight the history of our town," Ginger said, tapping her fingertips in thought. "We could group floats depicting different eras. For example, the original settling of Summer Beach, the official founding a century ago, the equestrian period, the surf culture boom, and today's innovations."

Marina pictured the colorful floats drifting down Main Street, cheered on by crowds of visitors and locals alike. She would add her flavored popcorn and centennial cupcakes to the food truck menu.

"We should get the schools involved," Kai said.

Bennett nodded. "The high school marching band and twirlers will be there."

"Axe and I could bring some young performers with us," Kai said. "We've been working with the school drama department on an upcoming musical."

Marina was impressed. "That's a great idea."

"We appreciate that, Kai." Bennett turned to her. "And Marina, would you consider taking charge of organizing the event? You have such a knack for bringing the community together, just as you've done here. Besides the parade, there are publicity and donations to manage. We have to organize retail and food vendors, a stage with performances, and old-fashioned races with prizes. While people on the committee are handling different events, all this requires coordination. What we need is a good general manager."

"I thought Rhoda was doing that," Marina said. While the event would be memorable, she was busy enough.

Bennett shook his head. "She's been called out of town on family matters. It's short notice, but given how well you run the Coral Cafe, schedule your food truck, and deal with customers, I could think of no one better."

"I've heard if you need a job done, ask the busiest person," Kai said. "They're the most organized."

Marina kicked Kai's foot under the table. With her full schedule, she didn't need such a ringing endorsement.

"My thought exactly," Bennett said. "Marina, will you consider supporting the community for this special event?"

"That's flattering, but I have a lot going on." Marina touched her temple. She'd already turned down this offer from Rhoda. Jack, Leo, Scout—those three were a handful. Would she have time for this?

"You would be marvelous," Ginger said. "Imagine the benefit to Summer Beach."

"Come on, Marina," Kai chimed in, kicking her back.

"It's a once-in-a-lifetime opportunity. Literally. You won't get another chance for a hundred years."

Heather paused at the table. "Without Rhoda involved, it sounds cool, Mom. You should do it. We'll all help, won't we?"

"Of course," Kai said, clapping her hands while Ginger nodded.

Gazing at the four expectant faces staring at her, Marina's resolve wavered. "I don't know," she said slowly.

She thought of Ginger and others who had contributed so much to making Summer Beach the place she loved today. Perhaps she owed a debt to the community as well. Could she really manage it? She would hate to be as ineffective as Rhoda.

$\mathcal{W}$hile Marina considered the offer, Ginger leaned forward, her eyes twinkling. "Perhaps Leo could ride with me in the parade. Mayor Bennett, if Leo is my plus-one, will there be room for him in the car? He could sit in the middle. I'm sure he would be thrilled."

Bennett beamed. Looking across the table, he said, "If you're in charge, we'll make room for Leo wherever she goes."

Marina hadn't expected the mayor and her grandmother to ante up a bargaining chip that would be so hard to refuse. "I'm sure Leo would be thrilled, but…"

Ginger reached for her hand. "You won't be alone in this. I can help you, as will Kai. And likely Brooke, too."

Kai beamed. "Put me down for the parade and entertainment."

"I realize how much this event means to everyone." Marina weighed the demands. Yet, she cared about Summer Beach, and she wanted residents and visitors to enjoy all the town had to offer.

Everyone was waiting for her answer.

Biting her lip, she decided. Somehow, she would make this happen.

"I appreciate your confidence in me," Marina said to Bennett. "And I'm happy to have the chance to contribute to the town that has made the Coral Cafe a success. When do I start?"

"Right now," he replied with a broad grin.

As they toasted with their water glasses and coffee cups, Cruise emerged from the kitchen. He balanced four plates of poached eggs, smoked salmon, and hollandaise sauce, each garnished with a generous dollop of glistening black caviar. Basil garnished a grilled tomato, and more caviar topped a grilled avocado filled with an infused aioli.

"I call this the mayor's special," he said as Heather helped him serve. "Eggs Benedict with a twist. Bon appétit."

Bennett thanked him. "What an honor. I didn't know this was on the menu."

"It's not," Marina said, inspecting the dish.

She didn't know that caviar had been on their supply list either. Langoustine, yes, but that was for the lunch special. He'd used a lot of caviar, more than what he should have if this were on the menu. Food costs were always a concern.

"Maybe it should be," Ginger said. "This is beautifully presented. Why, my old friend Julia Child would have been proud."

"Hey, you can call it the Mayor Eggs Bennett," Kai said, laughing at her own joke.

"It looks delicious," Marina said.

Still, Cruise didn't need to impress Bennett. He should be grilling the langoustine for the lunch special. He knew this; she planned the specials a week in advance.

"Thank you, that means a lot to me." Cruise smiled

humbly with his hands clasped behind his back. After darting a look at Marina, he added, "I'd better get back to work."

As they ate, the conversation about the centennial event and parade continued. Marina's mind was already racing ahead, compiling a mental list of everything she would need to pull off the celebration. She'd have to review schedules and road closures. Recruit volunteers from community groups. Talk to vendors about setting up booths.

Marina listened to ideas around the table. Turning to Bennett, she asked, "Is there a budget for all this?"

Bennett cleared his throat. "That's another very important task we need help with. I'm afraid Rhoda didn't get around to securing sponsors. Still, we have a small budget that will cover a brief fireworks show. Not much else, I'm afraid."

Marina gave a small sigh. *And secure sponsors to help fund it all*, she added to her mental list. She had already committed, but she wished she'd known about this.

Ginger touched her hand as if to reassure her. "I can call on Carol Reston and Hal."

"It's asking a lot, and so late," Marina said. "I should go with you." The Grammy Award-winning couple were locals, so everyone asked them for donations. She could approach Tyler and Celia, the retired tech couple who generously supported the school music program. Marina would have many calls to make.

Kai snapped her fingers. "I can trade Poppy Bay season tickets at the Seashell for some marketing help."

Marina smiled at her sister's exuberance. "You already did that to bring in Seabreeze Inn guests. Besides, with the new theater, you and Axe need the ticket sales."

Ginger reached across the table and patted Marina's

hand. "Don't fret, dear. I can help by calling in a few favors. I'll set up some meetings for us. It's time you met more of my friends anyway."

"I appreciate that," Marina said.

Despite her resolve, her stomach twisted with anxiety. What on earth did she just get herself into? She saw her free time with Jack suddenly evaporating. Yet, he was investigating that story for his editor. Maybe it was just as well they hadn't planned anything for their anniversary. Jack would understand. It wouldn't be for long; the centennial was only weeks away.

Marina glanced over her shoulder. A crowd was gathering at the entrance, but Heather had disappeared. That wasn't like her.

Frowning, Marina said, "Excuse me, I need to check on Heather and lunch."

"Thank you all," Bennett said, rising. "I'll set up a planning meeting."

Marina hurried toward the kitchen. Heather was just coming out, and her face was even paler than it had been a few minutes ago.

Stopping her, Marina said, "You don't look well, darling."

"I feel sick." Heather pressed a hand to her stomach. "Mom, I'm not sure I can handle the lunch business."

"Go upstairs and go to bed. We'll manage." Marina hesitated, lowering her voice. "What did you have to eat?"

"Only the langoustine and eggs. Oh, Mom, I'm so sorry, but I think I'm going to—" She cupped her hand over her mouth.

"Go now," Marina said, a sinking feeling growing inside. "I'll send Ginger after you."

Heather rushed toward the cottage while Marina strode

into the kitchen, signaling Ginger on her way. Cruise was at the refrigerator.

She pressed her palms on the counters. "Let me see the langoustine right now."

Grumbling, Cruise acquiesced.

Marina touched a piece. Her heart sank. "It's warm, which means it has been unrefrigerated for a long time. It was out when I asked you if you'd put it up, wasn't it?"

"I meant to. I just got busy."

"Yet you had time to create special dishes for Heather and the mayor." Marina couldn't listen to excuses, not with patrons lining up at the front for tables. "We can't serve the langoustine. Heather is sick from it."

"It might not be that."

Shaking her head, she took the seafood and dumped it into the trash. "Take that out, please."

Cruise threw down a towel. "You didn't have to do that. I know how to handle seafood."

"Maybe you do, but this time, you were distracted. We can't take a chance. This is unacceptable."

Cruise cursed and banged a spatula on the stove.

This was a crisis, and Marina didn't have time to argue. Every week, she sent out a newsletter with the daily specials. "Soon, we'll have patrons who are coming for the langoustine salad."

"I'll come up with something else."

"At this point, I'd rather you stick to the menu."

Again, Cruise turned away, grumbling.

Marina's patience was wearing thin. "Look, I know you're here for the summer surfing. But you need to take your mind off the waves and focus on your job. A few cases of food poisoning can kill a restaurant in a small town. And today's profits are literally in the can—along with the cost of that caviar I didn't authorize. We've talked about food costs. Ingredients like that are fun to work with, but this isn't a hotel with deep pockets."

Cruise's face reddened. "How is Heather?"

"Probably throwing up." Marina turned on the sink to wash her hands. "Erase the langoustine salad from the specials board and take out the trash."

A trace of remorse shaded his face. "You're not going to check on her?"

Marina wished she could, but she had to contain this situation. "I sent her grandmother. We have a lunch crowd to serve, so get moving. I'll put on the soup and start seating people."

Cruise stuck out his chin. "I know you don't believe me, but there was nothing wrong with that langoustine. I know my way around kitchens, and I've been trying to prove it to you. You saw my Eggs Benedict. That was a masterpiece."

"Cruise, I appreciate your effort, although it takes more than a dollop of costly caviar to make a chef. And we don't have time for this."

The line at the front was growing longer, and anxiety swirled within her. One man she didn't recognize was looking particularly antsy. He kept checking his cufflinks and straightening the collar of his jacket. He looked nervous and slightly out of place, as if he were visiting from the city. He looked familiar, but Marina couldn't place him.

Was he the food critic Rhoda had mentioned? Her heart sank.

Today, of all days.

"You're too cheap to hire the staff you need," Cruise continued, his tone taking on a sarcastic edge.

Marina was appalled at his comment. "I have a real

budget to consider. The cafe isn't like the luxury hotels you've worked at."

He narrowed his eyes. "Maybe I shouldn't have left."

Anger tightened her chest. Marina lifted a pot onto the stove and turned on the flame. She had to be decisive and act swiftly.

"You're probably right," she said, measuring her words. "Because your attitude isn't a good fit here. Goodbye, Cruise. I'll mail your final check."

His mouth dropped open. "You just made a big mistake." Cruise tore off his apron and strode out the rear entrance.

Marina heaved a sigh. Maybe she had. Good help was hard to find in the summer, but she would not put up with insolence, especially with the centennial looming ahead. Cruise was young and talented, but he still had a lot to learn. She needed people who were willing to pull together.

A kitchen was no place for attitude, as her first restaurant manager had drilled into the team. This wasn't a reality show; it was her life and livelihood.

She hurried toward the front entry. The line was growing longer.

Kai stopped her. "What happened back there?" she whispered. "I saw you and Cruise arguing."

That scene might make the gossip rounds, she thought with dismay. "Heather is sick, and I had to fire Cruise."

After years in high-pressure television, she had learned the ability to make decisions was crucial. She would not risk the health of her customers, many of whom were older. It was a shame because Cruise was talented, but he still had a lot to learn.

"I'll handle the front," Kai said, looking back at the growing line.

"But your appointment…"

"It can wait. This is an emergency." Kai gestured toward people who were looking frustrated with the lack of service. "Go take care of your kitchen."

"Thanks," Marina said. "And erase the langoustine salad from the specials board. Tell anyone who asks that we didn't receive the shipment."

"You got it." Kai paused, biting her lip. "Sorry if I pushed the centennial on you. I didn't know you were having kitchen problems."

"I'll figure it out. The centennial is something I want to do." Glancing at the line at the entry, Marina touched Kai's shoulder and lowered her voice. "See that man by himself? The one adjusting his cuffs and looking perturbed?"

Kai spotted him. "What do you want me to do, boss lady?"

"Make sure he gets good service. He might be a food critic that Rhoda sent." As if she didn't have enough to worry about right now.

"Will do. Tell me everything later." Kai whisked away in a blaze of pink, her heels tapping on the wooden deck. She picked up a stack of menus for patrons and turned her megawatt smile onto Mr. Cufflinks. "Welcome to the Coral Cafe. Thanks for waiting. How many in your party?"

Marina breathed a sigh of relief. With Kai at her side, she could handle this. This reminded her of when she'd first opened the cafe.

Although she trusted Ginger, she was worried about Heather. When she returned to the kitchen, she quickly tapped a message to her.

Let me know how Heather is doing. If she worsens, she might need to see a doctor. I suspect food poisoning. Be there as soon as I can.

The smell of charred food seeped from the oven. Marina yanked out a pan of burned bread Cruise had left.

She pressed a hand to her forehead. With Cruise gone, she didn't know how she would manage the centennial now. But she'd made a promise to the mayor, and Summer Beach needed her. She would have to hire other help as fast as she could.

When Kai pinned the possible food critic's order onto the stainless-steel wheel, Marina took special care to make it perfect. She shuddered to think what might have happened if he'd contracted food poisoning. Relieved that disaster had been averted for now, she kept working.

When Kai came into the kitchen to retrieve the order, she had an odd look on her face. "Mr. Cufflinks just asked if Cruise worked here."

Marina's heart quickened. "What did you tell him?"

"I said Cruise wasn't here, and I asked him how he knew him. The guy said he'd followed his career, but then he changed the subject. I couldn't get any more information out of him unless I tackled him. I figured that wouldn't be appropriate."

"So, he's probably the food critic. Maybe he reviewed a restaurant Cruise had worked in, and he was expecting him here."

Kai picked up the order. "Here goes. I hope he likes it."

Had she been overly hasty in firing Cruise? Maybe, but she had to protect her customers, and she would make the same decision again. She hoped Heather was doing okay; she would check on her as soon as she could.

Marina looked out over the dining patio, watching Kai deliver the man's order. Still, something didn't seem quite right.

Maybe Kai could glean more information from him.

8

*M*arina smoothed tendrils of Heather's hair from her face. She had been worried about her daughter all day. She checked on her after the lunch rush, and Ginger had given her updates all day. "How are you feeling now?"

"Still queasy." Heather eased up in bed. "I need to get better so I can watch Blake and his team release the sea lions."

"I don't think you're going anywhere just yet." Marina fluffed a stack of white cotton pillows behind her daughter's head and perched beside her. "Blake is awfully nice, though. Maybe he'll wait for you to release them."

Heather gave a shy smile. "Maybe."

Marina waited, but her daughter didn't elaborate on Blake. "Do you think you can eat some broth or soup? You haven't had anything since breakfast."

"I've had gallons of liquids." Heather cupped her hands around a cup of tea. "Broth sounds okay, but not right now. Stay with me?" She leaned her head on Marina's shoulder.

"Of course, sweetheart."

They sat in companionable silence in Brooke's old room that Heather had claimed in Ginger's beach house. It was down the hall from rooms where Marina and Kai had spent a significant part of their lives.

Like their old rooms, this sunny bedroom had an iron bed covered with a white chenille bedspread. Pastel beach glass and weathered driftwood filled glass jars. These were remnants of beach walks from years gone by. And as in Marina's old room, one of Ginger's sweet, coded cipher borders decorated these walls, too.

Heather looked up from her tea. "Mom, you didn't have to fire Cruise."

"I see word travels fast." Marina smoothed a hand over her daughter's thick hair.

Heather shrugged. "Was what he did really so bad?"

"Raw langoustine cannot be left unrefrigerated. I was worried that you'd have to go to the hospital for food poisoning. You were quite sick, darling."

"I'll be okay. And I'm not so sure it was the langoustine. Maybe I picked up a virus at school. A lot of kids have been sick."

Marina pressed her hand against Heather's forehead. "You haven't run a fever."

"I felt warm earlier. Can you let Cruise come back? He's part of the team, and he needs work. He doesn't have any family to support him. And I like working with him."

"I understand, but many people could have become ill because of his negligence. It's nice of you to defend him, but actions have consequences. We have a lot of older customers who might not have rebounded as you have. Food poisoning can be very serious."

"Maybe it wasn't the langoustine. He thinks you probably could have served it."

Marina drew in a sharp breath. "I couldn't take that chance in the business. And I'd still like for you to see a doctor."

"No," Heather blurted. "I mean, I know I'm fine. Or I will be. I felt funny even before I had the langoustine and eggs. Maine-style, that's what Cruise called the omelet he made for me. Like his grandpa used to make for him. It was so good, and I thought it might settle my stomach."

Marina rubbed her daughter's shoulder. "Guess it did the opposite."

"He might have to leave Summer Beach."

"That might be a good idea for him."

Heather picked at threads on the bedspread. "But I really like him, Mom."

Something in Heather's voice struck a chord in Marina. "Have you been dating?"

With a shrug, Heather replied, "Not really. But we hung out some."

Marina wasn't sure what that meant, but she didn't want to come out too strong against Cruise and force Heather to choose sides. She wondered about Blake, but that choice was up to her daughter.

"Cruise is talented, though he still has a lot to learn," Marina said. "Many young men mature later than women."

Heather bristled at that. "We're not kids, Mom."

"I won't rehire him, if that's what this is about." Marina kissed Heather's forehead and stood. "I'll heat some broth for you."

Ginger appeared in the doorway. "I'll see to that," she said. "You should go home. You have an early day tomorrow."

"Thanks, I will." Without Cruise, Marina had a lot of prep work to do. After hugging Heather and Ginger, she made her way downstairs. She had already told Jack she would be late for dinner.

Before she left, she walked across the property to the cafe and went through the kitchen to the small room she used for her office. She had promised Cruise she'd mail his final check.

Marina flipped on her computer and opened her payroll software. "Let's see...where are you, C.M.," she said to herself, going through the list. Cruise was only a nickname.

She filled in the final amount with a few taps, turned to the printer, and inserted a blank check. After printing, she tucked the check into an envelope, stamped it, and turned off the computer.

As she did, she had a nagging feeling. She liked Cruise, but sometimes losing a job was a wake-up call. He was creative and good with food, but this wasn't the place for him. Not for long, anyway. Someday, he might well surpass her abilities.

She realized she didn't know much about Cruise. Aside from his prior work experience, he never spoke of his family.

Maybe there was a reason for that. A twinge of guilt tweaked her neck.

Heather had told her he really needed this job. While Marina had corrected him numerous times, would once more have mattered? She didn't like terminating an employee.

Yet, with his skills, he should be able to get another position soon.

She shut the door to the cafe behind her.

Outside, she got into her turquoise Mini Cooper, put the

top down, and drove along the beach road toward home. Fortunately, it was just minutes from Ginger's.

Heather preferred staying at the cottage, saying she had more autonomy with Ginger. Marina understood that.

Her grandmother was in good health, but she felt better that Heather was with her to help with household tasks and lift heavy items. Ginger was fiercely independent. She had a mind of her own; always had, always would.

After parking in the garage, Marina climbed the rear steps and opened the door. "Something smells delicious."

Jack was at the stove ladling the marinara sauce she'd made last night over pasta. His startling blue eyes still took her breath away.

He rested the ladle on a ceramic spoon rest, wrapped his arms around her, and kissed her. "I'm glad you're home. You sure had a tough day. Wish you had called me earlier to clean tables for you."

"Kai was there, and she swept to the rescue." Marina had called him after lunch to tell him what had happened with Cruise and her new work on the centennial event.

"You have a lot to handle now," Jack said. "How soon do you think you can hire new help?"

"I had a couple of part-timers last summer. I'll see if they're available."

Just then, Scout slid around the corner into the kitchen with Leo in pursuit. The boy flung his arms around her.

"Hey, you," Marina said, laughing. She hugged Leo and then scratched the scruff of Scout's neck. The dog's tongue lolled out in a happy grin.

"Aren't you eating a little late?" she asked.

"We had ice cream sundaes," Leo said.

Jack grinned. "We saw Samantha and her parents in the village. They invited us to join them for a couple of scoops."

Marina took flatware from a drawer and set the kitchen table while Jack ladled the pasta and sauce onto plates.

"Sure is nice to have someone make dinner," Marina said.

"I'm trying," Jack said. "I'm glad you're counting warming up leftovers as cooking."

"That's why I make extra," she said, giving him another kiss.

Once they were seated, Marina turned to Leo. "I have a surprise. The mayor came by the cafe to ask Ginger to be the Grand Marshal for the centennial parade and celebration."

"That's a real honor," Jack said, smiling. "She'll be great."

"What's a cententacle?" Leo asked, stumbling over the word.

Jack laughed. "That's centennial, my little guy. One hundred years ago, folks got together, created this town, and called it Summer Beach."

Leo screwed up his face, which was already splattered with tomato sauce. "What was it called before?"

"I have no idea." Jack grinned as he wound pasta onto his fork. "I don't have all the answers, son."

"And there's more," Marina said, passing Leo a napkin. "Kai and Axe are performing in the parade, and Bennett asked me to oversee the event committee."

Jack rested his hand on hers. "Are you sure you'll have time now?"

"I committed to him before I let Cruise go, so I'll have to make it work."

"Where did you let Cruise go?" Leo asked.

Jack leaned toward him. "That's a figure of speech, son."

Leo looked even more puzzled. "What's that?"

When Jack looked helpless to answer, Marina chuckled. "Just something people say. Cruise doesn't work at the cafe anymore."

"Can I be in the parade?" Leo asked.

"That's the surprise," Marina replied. "Bennett and Ginger plan to ride in his wife Ivy's vintage Chevrolet convertible with her at the front of the parade, which is a huge honor. Since there's an extra spot in the car, Ginger thought you might like to join her."

Leo bounced in his chair. "I want to do that."

"That was nice of Ginger," Jack said. "I know how busy you are. Need me to help with the event?"

"I don't think so. Ginger and Kai promised to pitch in." She told Jack and Leo about what people were doing for the parade. "A lot of people building floats or decorating vintage cars."

Jack stared at her for a moment. "Hey, how about we decorate the old VW van for the parade. It's plenty vintage."

"I want to help," Leo said.

Jack bumped Leo's fist. "Looks like Rocinante rides again."

Marina gave him a small kiss, smiling at Jack's nickname for his old VW van—a name he'd borrowed from two writers, Cervantes, and later, Steinbeck. "Can you manage with that story you're working on?"

Marina knew how much this article meant to him; it was the first he'd written since he'd arrived in Summer Beach. She didn't want him to get caught up in the centennial and miss his deadline.

"I have a lot of research and writing to do, but I'll manage with Leo's help. Right, sport?"

"We sure will," Leo added, beaming with expectation.

Jack touched her shoulder. "We're a family now, and we'll do this together. We'll help you, too."

A slight twinge of guilt tweaked the back of Marina's neck as she realized her oversight. She should include Jack and Leo in her activities if they wanted. Blending their family was important. She'd been single for so long.

Yet she loved Jack dearly and adored Leo. Getting married was the easy part. Adjusting to one another, including children and extended family, and still making time for romance in their relationship was another matter.

"On second thought, I'm sure I'll need some help along the way," Marina said, hugging Jack. "I couldn't do this without you and Leo."

She had no idea how she would juggle everything, but somehow, she would make it work. Maybe she needed their help after all.

9

*J*ack followed the old car in front of him. When it stopped at a light, he drew alongside it. "Pull over at that parking lot. We need to talk."

After easing to a stop, Jack slipped a small device into his pocket. He got out of his van and approached the other man's car. The last thing he wanted was this guy creeping around his home or this town. He motioned for Chaz to roll down his window. Jack folded his arms on the edge of the door.

He glanced behind him to see if anyone was watching. "I saw you coming out of the Coral Cafe. What are you doing in Summer Beach, and what did you want there?"

"If you must know, I was dining. Rather well, too. Although it could have been better."

Jack let that go. Was Chaz aware of his connection with the cafe? His being here was more than a coincidence. Still, he wouldn't let on that it was his wife's business on the chance that Chaz didn't know. Jack had meant to stop by for lunch with Marina, but when he saw the other man exiting the cafe, he'd immediately followed him.

Jack pressed him again. "What do you want from me?"

"Have you made those contacts I suggested?"

"I have."

One was a woman who had been wrongfully terminated from one of the oldest wealth management companies in the country, and she was willing to talk. Jack wasn't even sure of the questions to ask, but he hadn't had to do much more than listen and ask the occasional question. It was as if she'd been expecting him. Or someone like him.

He recalled her words. *I have a noncompete clause. So I can't work at the only profession I know. That's wrong, especially after what happened.* Then she launched into her story, which wasn't remarkable, except for the knowledge she'd gained into brilliant financial movements.

If she hadn't been unjustly fired, this story might have never come his way.

As for the other contact, Jack had reached out, but someone that important had others to return his calls. He didn't expect to hear from him without putting forth more effort.

Chaz stared ahead. "Your coverage will result in an investigation, so I am putting my affairs in order."

"You don't mean that." Jack was surprised. "You've finally returned, and this is what you're planning?"

"Don't be so dramatic. One might make arrangements for any number of reasons. Long journeys, for example."

Jack had no idea what the other man meant by that. Maybe Chaz took pleasure in teasing him. Still, Jack was connecting the clues, and the emerging picture was fascinating.

"You shouldn't be in Summer Beach," Jack said.

"I have as much right to be here enjoying the scenery as you."

"You know what I mean."

"A person can get lost in a small town like Summer Beach. Is that why you're here, Jack?"

"That's none of your business."

"But this is such a small world." A smile curved his lips. "Your wife's cafe is charming, by the way. I wouldn't have guessed." He punched a button on the door, and the window began to slide up.

Jack reached inside and stopped it. "Don't threaten my wife."

"Never. I am still a gentleman, regardless of my unfortunate change of residence."

"Then why are you here?"

"Coincidences are real," Chaz replied thoughtfully. "Life is littered with small ones that we take for granted. Your old friend John comes to mind and the phone rings. It's him. Or maybe you run into him on the street in a city of millions. But a major coincidence? Those we question."

They were getting somewhere now. "Give me an example."

Chaz shook his head. "You'll find it. You can trust me now, Jack, though you will find that hard to believe."

"Why should I?"

The other man sighed. "Because I don't want anything from you. It was a nice gesture for you to pick up the check at lunch, but unnecessary."

"You want me to write a story."

"Whether it is published or not, the process has been set in motion. Goodbye, Jack."

Jack stepped back, irritated at the encounter and the lack of information. Would he ever lead a normal life, or was he destined to carry his past and the characters he'd met with him for the rest of his life?

He'd told himself this would be his last assignment. Yet, he enjoyed the intellectual stimulation in the pursuit of truth. Could he continue this work from Summer Beach without endangering his family?

Jack didn't know the answer to that. He returned to his van, got in, and flicked off the small recording device.

As he turned back toward the cottage, he tried to put himself into Chaz's situation. What would the other man want at this phase of his life?

He was no longer welcome in the esteemed society he was once part of. That life would remain forever beyond his reach. His family had disowned him, his wife divorced him before she died, and somewhere he had a son who wanted no part of him.

Was it revenge? Jack couldn't identify any direct link between Chaz's leads and his former life. The *why* of all this eluded him. That was what Jack found the most frustrating. Once he connected the reasons for people's actions, the story would generally fall into place. Greed, revenge, and even lust were the usual motivations.

But Chaz? His crime was being a partner to the wrong man, Charles Bennington, his wife's father. Jack drummed his fingers on the steering wheel, thinking about what he recalled of the strange story.

Chaz, born Charles Milford Smith, had taken his wife's name upon their marriage, becoming Charles Bennington-Smith, and eventually dropping the Smith part of the name. Many people assumed he was the senior's son. From what Jack had heard, Chaz seldom corrected them, nor did the father-in-law.

Jack knew why Chaz didn't talk about it. His family had

lost everything during a real estate crash, and his father blamed him for not being there to help, even though he was studying at Princeton University.

Throughout his partnership with the senior Bennington, Chaz had frequently signed documents, seldom questioning his father-in-law's actions. He'd enjoyed the good life, never imagining the privileged life he managed to land in might come to an end.

Or maybe he had, and it hit too close to home.

As he'd told Jack years ago during the trial, if he questioned too much, he stood to lose everything. He followed his father-in-law's lead until everything crumbled around him.

Jack hadn't thought much of Chaz before, but now, he was an intriguing character, if only because Jack couldn't figure out his present motive.

A timer on his phone dinged, and Jack realized he had half an hour before an important call. He no longer had time to visit the cafe.

He turned back toward home, still turning over the conversation with Chaz as he drove. What had the guy meant by coincidences?

10

When Marina stood, everyone in the community room at City Hall applauded.

"Thank you," she said, raising her hand in appreciation. "I know we're all eager to get to work. Most of you know my grandmother, Ginger Delavie, who will serve as the Grand Marshal this year."

Cheers rang out. Seated in the front row, Ginger stood and turned, waving at her friends. Kai and Axe sat with her.

However, Heather had stayed at home. Although she was feeling better, she said she was tired. When Marina arrived at the cottage to check on her, she overheard her talking to Blake on the phone. Maybe that had something to do with her daughter's decision to stay home.

Marina thanked the crowd for coming. "This will be a huge festival for Summer Beach that will bring many visitors, which is good for our economy. And as my sister Kai says, it's a once-in-a-lifetime event. Our grandchildren and great-grandchildren will likely be organizing the next one.

So, take lots of photos for them. Who wants to be the official photographer?"

Everyone laughed at that, and a young man waved his hand. Jack took his name, jotting it down on a clipboard.

The room was crowded tonight. The mayor sat with their friends Jen and George from the hardware store, who wore their usual jeans and denim jackets. Jack sat with Vanessa's friends, John and Denise, whose daughter Samantha was Leo's best friend. Near them were Leilani and Roy Miyake from the Hidden Garden nursery, where Marina and Ginger bought their plants.

Cookie O'Toole, the round-faced organizer in charge of the farmers market was there. So was Rosa, who owned the first food truck in Summer Beach, Rosa's Tacos. Both women were eager to be involved, but they didn't get along.

Marina hoped they'd get along tonight.

She looked at the agenda she had prepared. "We have a great deal to cover today. First, if you've already volunteered for a task, raise your hand. Jack will pass around a volunteer sign-up sheet. We'll need your name, what you want to do, and your contact information."

Cookie's hand shot up. "I'm overseeing the food vendors."

"No, she's not," Rosa said, waving from the other side. "I'm doing that."

Marina glanced at the mayor for help, but Bennett only shrugged. "Did Rhoda resolve this before she left?"

"She told me that I could manage it this time," Rosa said.

"We're not taking turns at events like kindergarteners," Cookie shot back. "I'm in charge. If anyone's managing food at this centennial, it should be someone who knows all the local vendors."

Rosa raised an eyebrow. "I know everyone in Summer Beach. More than just those at the farmers market."

The old rivalry was still alive.

"Ladies," she said, intervening. "We value both of you. Let's collaborate. Rosa, your expertise in fast food service will be essential. And Cookie, your connections with the local vendors will be invaluable. You're both co-chairs."

Cookie and Rosa exchanged glances. Marina hoped to see traces of mutual respect, but there was nothing.

"I can't work with her," Cookie complained.

"It's that, or I'll find someone entirely new to handle this." Marina pressed her lips together and waited.

She'd heard about their feud but didn't know what was behind it. It seemed Cookie had barred Rosa from bringing her food truck to the farmers market or having a stall there. In retaliation, Rosa parked the food truck near an entrance.

"Okay, okay," Cookie said, casting a disparaging look at Rosa, who looked equally perturbed. "We'll work together."

Rosa and Cookie grudgingly accepted this, but Marina had a feeling this wasn't the last she'd hear of this.

The first crisis averted, Marina thought. "Next up, the parade organization. Entrants and order of the parade. Who is working on that?"

Jen stood up. "George and I can contribute to a team effort. And we'll volunteer our time to help those who are building floats. Come see us at Nailed It for a consultation."

"Sounds fancy; thank you, Jen." Marina was relieved someone other than her would keep that schedule.

Kai leaned over and spoke to her husband. Axe stood, his cowboy boots adding even more height to his long frame. "My construction team can also advise on technical issues. Mind if we work together?"

"We'd welcome that," Jen said, while George nodded.

Another resident raised his hand. "How is the order decided?"

Jen turned to him. "We'll look at the entrants and see what makes sense."

The man continued, "I've donated a lot of money to the committee, so I should be first in line."

Marina saw Jack stifle a laugh. "And everyone who participates will appreciate your generosity. But that spot is traditionally reserved for the Grand Marshal and the Mayor."

Again, Kai and Axe conferred. This time, Kai turned to Jen. "We can help organize the order in the parade. It's like directing a show."

"And we all know how good you are at that." Marina nodded to Kai, Axe, Jen, and George. "You're the parade committee. Get together and sort it out."

Feeling a small measure of relief, Marina tapped her list. "Now for the school participants, the marching band, dance team, and twirlers."

A group of teachers and school board representatives were handling that, and they seemed organized. She made notes of names and responsibilities. "Plus the 4-H Club and the Summer Beach Homecoming Court."

Marina looked up. "What else am I leaving out?"

"We'd be happy to participate," Leilani said. Seated next to her, her husband Roy nodded in agreement.

Another woman stood. "And the Coastal Surf Club. We're building a float."

Others joined in with more comments until Marina could hardly keep up. This was a larger job than the mayor had let on. She cast a desperate look at Jack, who was taking notes.

"Need some help?" Jack asked softly.

"Sure do." Marina turned back to the crowd. "If you have any other questions, direct them to my new assistant, Jack Ventana. He'll make a note of them."

Several people began talking at once to Jack, and he held up his hands. "One at a time, folks."

"I'll help," Ginger said. Several people turned to her to discuss ideas.

Marina stayed on to answer questions and learn what residents could offer. She was pleased to meet quite a few new people.

After the meeting, people trickled out until only Jack and Ginger were left. Marina and Jack had agreed to take Ginger home.

As they walked out, Marina asked Ginger, "What's behind the situation between Cookie and Rosa?"

"Looked like a fierce food competition to me," Jack said.

Ginger shook her head. "That stems from an old jealousy that has nothing to do with food. They both dated the same young man in high school."

"Wait a minute—high school?" Marina wondered if she had heard that correctly. "Their feud goes back thirty years?"

"More," Ginger replied. "They're hardly spring chickens."

Marina shook her head. "Now, why did I volunteer for this?"

"Because you enjoy being a part of the community, dear," Ginger said.

Jack tapped his clipboard. "We still have tasks no one signed up for."

She turned to Ginger. "Could we have a coordinating meeting tomorrow? I'll ask Kai, too. If we pool our resources and contacts, we can pull off this event."

"I'm happy to help," Ginger said. "We can accomplish more together."

Jack put his arm around Marina. "Count me in, too."

"I appreciate that," she replied, recalling their conversation. "We're a team. But you've been working late an awful lot." How could she turn down his offer?

Ginger's voice cut through her thoughts. "Jack, you told me you have an important story to finish for your editor. As well as the illustrations for our collaboration."

"That's true, but—"

"We can manage without you," Ginger said. "Once you're finished, your input will be welcome." She turned to Marina. "Sometimes, being a team means recognizing your teammate has other responsibilities and carrying the burden without them for a while."

"Ginger is right," he said slowly. "I'm almost finished, and this will give me strong motivation to wrap it up."

Marina was relieved. "Afterward, you pick up the slack on the centennial. I promise there will still be plenty to do."

"My granddaughter has a point," Ginger said. "Tend to your business first. As for you," she added, looking at Marina. "You need to hire dependable help right away."

"First thing in the morning." Marina smiled at Jack. She would breathe easier once he completed his article.

Ginger smiled with satisfaction. "I'll see you at the cafe in the morning, and after we've sorted out lunch, I'll meet with Jack on our book project."

Once they arrived at the Coral Cottage, Ginger turned to them. "Jack, dear, would you help me fetch some boxes from the attic? I found some items that will prove useful for the centennial. The cartons are too heavy for me, and Heather still isn't feeling well."

Marina was still upset with Cruise for serving Heather

tainted food. Her daughter was feeling better, but food poisoning could wreak havoc on a person's system for some time.

"Happy to help," Jack said, following Ginger upstairs.

Marina followed to check on Heather. She cracked the door to Heather's room, but her daughter was fast asleep. She shut the door quietly.

Jack had already climbed into the attic ahead of her. Ginger was telling him which boxes she wanted.

While Marina waited for him to pass boxes down to her, she stopped by the bathroom in the hallway.

The vintage wallpaper was a faded floral pattern Ginger chose years ago. The air inside smelled faintly of lavender that Ginger brought from the garden.

Marina was about to leave when she caught the reflection of a pregnancy test kit in the mirror on the countertop behind a stack of towels. Kai must have left it, she figured.

But why would she hide it? And why would she have brought it here?

At once, Marina knew whose it was.

That wasn't Kai's. It had to belong to Heather.

Marina winced at the thought. Every talk she'd had with her daughter about being careful and not limiting her future came rushing back. Heather had listened and agreed. But this was clear evidence that her daughter had made a mistake. And then, with a sinking feeling, Marina thought about Cruise.

No wonder Heather had been upset over his firing.

And no wonder she didn't want to see a doctor for her food poisoning. Because that probably wasn't why she couldn't keep food down.

Marina picked up the small box. She hadn't been snooping, but Heather might take it that way. Or worse, deny it.

She looked at the front of the package. *Three tests inside,* it said. The flap was open, and she looked inside. One test was missing.

Automatically, she checked the trashcan, but it was empty. She considered that. If a test was negative, a woman would discard it. But if it was positive, she might keep it for evidence. To show another person...to prove it to her partner.

Marina closed her eyes, realizing the validity of this reasoning. She pressed a hand to her face, feeling sick about this. Heather and Cruise weren't in love, and a child would complicate their young lives.

But she would have to be there for Heather.

On impulse, Marina took one test from the box and slipped it into her pocket. She needed her evidence, too.

11

*I*t was still dark outside when Jack's alarm buzzed. He shut it off, kissed Marina, and rose to make coffee. He could sleep later, but his internal clock was still set to East Coast time.

He'd also had difficulty adjusting to the quietness of Summer Beach when he arrived here. Accustomed to the sounds of the city, he compensated by sleeping with the windows cracked, letting in the distant roar of crashing waves and the squawks of seagulls. The ocean breeze was invigorating, and he did his best work in the stillness of the morning after Marina left to open the cafe and after his run on the beach.

Scout trotted after him, his toenails clicking on the hard-wood floors as he kept pace with Jack.

"Hey, old boy. Fresh water for you?"

Scout wagged his tail in reply.

Jack tapped the button on the coffee maker, which they always set up the night before. While the water gurgled in the machine, he rinsed out Scout's bowl and refilled it.

While Scout lapped his water, Jack watched the coffee and considered his day ahead. He was determined to make headway on the leads Chaz provided to connect the story. Details were beginning to fall into place, and he had managed to contact others who corroborated the woman's statements.

Vast sums of money were being moved around the globe, ostensibly via investments. *Look for the source*, his contact told him. Her knowledge went far, but he still had missing pieces. He still wondered what Chaz was doing in Summer Beach at the Coral Cafe.

He heard Marina behind him and turned, opening his arms to her. "Good morning, sweetheart." She wore a short nightgown nearly as soft as her skin.

"Same to you, honey," she said, nestling into his embrace. "You're awfully warm."

Holding her, a thought occurred to him. "Do you believe in coincidences?"

She gave him a lazy smile. "If that's what you want to call them."

"Is that a *yes*?"

Marina ran a hand through her hair. "Isn't it awfully early for this?"

"I'm just wondering what people mean by that."

As the coffee gurgled to completion, he brought out two cups and poured their coffee, while Marina brought cream from the refrigerator and splashed just the right amount in each one.

With her hands curled around her cup, she leaned against the counter. "One could argue that everything in life is a coincidence. Or that things are meant to be. But who really knows?"

Jack nodded, grasping her meaning. "You sound like Ginger."

"I'll take that as a compliment."

He sipped his coffee, then asked, "Do you think there's much difference between small coincidences and major ones?"

"Little ones are amusing. What do you mean by major ones?"

"I'm not sure."

She smiled sleepily. "Maybe those are what people call blessings or destiny."

"Or incredible luck," he added.

"I suppose it all depends on a person's point of view." Marina kissed him. "Would you call how we met a coincidence?"

Grinning, Jack stroked her shoulder. "I call it the luckiest day of my life. Hey, don't we have an anniversary coming up?"

Marina's eyes twinkled over the rim of her coffee cup. "It's the same day as the centennial."

"Another coincidence." Jack laughed, but he wanted to think of something special to commemorate it. "Anything special you want to do?"

"I think we can rule out dinner at Beaches," she said, smiling.

"That's the place of no coincidences." He'd missed a date with her there once and bungled another.

"We'll think of something," she said, kissing him before she left the kitchen.

He watched her go, thinking again how lucky he was to have found her. And he would do anything to protect her.

. . .

After seeing Marina off and working all morning, Jack drove to Ginger's cottage and walked toward the entryway of her well-maintained home. A wooden swing was positioned on the front porch with a view of the sea, where the rhythmic sound of waves provided a calming backdrop.

Yet, his mind was anything but calm. The deeper he delved into the information Chaz provided, the more concerned he grew.

What he'd pieced together and confirmed this morning had led him to call his editor and bring in a colleague, another investigative journalist. He needed help, and he knew when to ask for it. Chaz was right; the story was in motion.

Jack decided this article would be his last one. He had a new life to live in Summer Beach.

When he stepped onto the porch, he noticed the door was slightly ajar. Touching the door lightly, he called out, "Ginger, are you here?"

Her voice floated out to him. "Come right in, dear."

She was expecting him. This was Summer Beach, after all. Some people didn't lock their doors or cars. Much like he had grown up on the farm, although if he'd done that in New York, he would have been robbed and laughed out of the city.

Jack knew the dangers of the work he did all too well. The closer he got to the truth, the more treacherous the path.

Exhaling a measure of relief, he went inside, automatically locking the door behind him. He followed the low strains of classical music that led him toward the library.

Inside, rich mahogany shelves that stretched from floor to ceiling were filled with leather-bound books. The room still held a faint aroma of pipe tobacco, though Ginger's husband Bertrand had passed away years before.

"You're right on time," Ginger said, rising to greet him with a kiss on each cheek.

"I wouldn't dream of insulting you by wasting your time."

She inclined her head. "Spending time with you is always a pleasure, my dear."

When working with Ginger, Jack had to bring his best game. Time was precious to her, and she did not suffer fools. Working with her was an exercise in skill and intellect.

"Please be seated." Ginger gestured to a club chair at a round table littered with sheets of his illustrations.

Jack sat at the table where they often met. Today, Ginger wore a taupe-colored linen dress with a polished brown kukui nut lei. A necklace once favored by Hawaiian royalty, he knew, and likely acquired during her far-flung travels.

Ginger tapped her fingers, studying him. "How is the work on your article going?"

"I made a good deal of progress this morning. I brought in a colleague to help with the research."

She nodded in satisfaction. "Glad to hear it. A balanced life is important."

He sensed what she was getting at. "I'm working on it. Marina and Leo mean everything to me."

"Even the best new marriages go through a period of adjustment." Her clear eyes shimmering with wisdom, she swiftly changed the subject. "I've been studying these illustrations you left with me."

Lacing his fingers, Jack leaned forward to wait for her judgment.

Ginger was the epitome of grace and sharper than most people half her age. Her hair was still tinted in a soft ginger shade from which she had derived her nickname decades ago. Even her granddaughters had been brought up to use that charming moniker. Yet her refined exterior was a mere sheath for her steely determination.

As he got to know Marina better, he saw Ginger's influence on her.

Ginger inspected his illustrations. "These are simply marvelous, Jack. The three young girls are adorable. They remind me so much of Marina, Brooke, and Kai when they were that age. You've done a fine job of capturing them again."

Jack smiled, feeling flattered. "Thank you, Ginger. I try my best to convey their essence."

"But right here, don't you think this one would be looking ahead with the other girls?"

"I assumed she might be glancing back at their dog."

Ginger considered that. "Yes, I see. Bring him into the picture, then."

"Of course."

A brief silence hung between them. However, Jack's thoughts were barely constrained. He wrestled with the urge to confide in Ginger, to seek her counsel on this matter pressing his conscience.

Why had he pitched this story? He'd danced around it for years before when the main players had been convicted and sent to prison. *Charles Bennington, the elder.* And Chaz. But this was a new angle and team. The former Ponzi scheme of wealth management theft paled in comparison.

He glanced around the room at the numerous accolades that spoke of Bertrand's career in diplomacy and Ginger's exploits in mathematics. Her love of puzzles and ciphers was everywhere—if you knew where to look.

A pair of needlework cushions held a message of love for

her late husband rendered in a cipher that looked like a vague pattern.

If there was anyone who could offer advice on a complex situation, it would be her.

She jotted notes on a notepad and handed it to him. "These changes will do. Then we can send the complete manuscript and illustrations to the editor."

"I'll turn that around right away." He shifted in his chair.

"Yes? You have something to add?" Ginger removed her reading glasses.

"If you have time. It's about the story."

She sat back and steepled her hands. "I do today, thank you for asking."

He could trust Ginger. She had never spoken of the sensitive information she had been privy to. Her stories revolved around her travels, parties, and fascinating people. She wouldn't divulge his secrets. Of course, he trusted Marina, but he didn't want to burden her with this. Or worry her. Yet.

Quickly, he laid bare the case he was investigating without naming names. A top-tier wealth management company with secret controlling members, a high-profile politician, a trail of foreign shell companies, and the concealment of unimaginable sums of money. Investment returns too good to be true, and a scheme as clever as it was dangerous.

Ginger absorbed it all, her gaze piercing yet understanding. "Fascinating. And quite challenging."

"I enjoy unraveling wrongdoing." Jack cleared his throat. "However, I have concerns. Personal concerns, that is."

"About your family."

Jack nodded. Marina, Leo, Heather, Ethan, and the rest of his family in Texas.

"Of course," she began, choosing her words carefully. "Sometimes the pursuit of truth is riddled with danger. But, with the right strategy and discretion, you can navigate even the most treacherous waters. Your duty is important, but your family is more so. Tread carefully, gather all the evidence, but ensure safeguards are in place."

"Would you continue if you were me?"

Ginger shook her head. "I cannot make your decisions, Jack. You're a smart man, so trust your instincts. They've served you well so far."

"Usually, yes."

"Then you'll know if you should back off."

Jack nodded, feeling his shoulders slightly lighter. Ginger's balanced perspective gave him direction. "Marina suspects that all is not right with this story."

"She has good instincts, and she's made of sterner stuff than you realize." Ginger reached for a pen and jotted a name on her pad. "This is a former colleague you may call on if needed."

"Like a lifeline?"

"Something like that." Ginger tore off the paper and handed it to him. "Use my name, of course. You are my grandson-in-law."

As he left, he realized he also needed to include Ginger in that protection. He was determined to uncover the truth while keeping his family safe. This story had become more than a paycheck or an education for Leo; it had renewed his passion for his expertise. Still, he'd have to watch his back.

And be aware of coincidences.

He would finalize his part and hand off the story as soon

as he could. Gus had agreed it was more involved than they'd realized and was already assembling a team.

The promises Jack made to Marina and Leo were important. He'd known colleagues who'd sacrificed marriages and relationships for their careers. At one time in his life, he had done that, too.

But not this time.

12

*A*s Marina cleaned the kitchen after lunch, she gave her newly hired team instructions. She was relieved that a sous chef she had employed last year was available. She had also called in a second young woman who had helped with a few catering jobs.

To manage the centennial celebration, she had to have help.

She wouldn't count on Heather as much as she had, especially since her daughter would return to school in the fall.

Yesterday, Heather had rushed out early to meet Blake, so she covered for her. The family of sea lions was being released, and Heather didn't want to miss it. Marina couldn't begrudge her daughter that. Besides, she liked Blake.

But then she thought of what she'd discovered in Heather's bathroom at Ginger's. She needed to find time to speak to her daughter alone. Hopefully, she could catch up with her later today. Heather had quickly disappeared after lunch.

Right now, Marina had to work on planning the centennial. She wouldn't let down the mayor or the residents of Summer Beach. This event would bring in many tourists and showcase their community's history and future. And as Ginger was fond of pointing out, it would be good for business.

The day was overcast, so many sun worshippers were probably shopping or pampering themselves. With the lunch rush over, the cafe was quieter than usual today, but Marina welcomed that. With her new team tending to the kitchen, she had asked Kai and Ginger to join her.

"Hello, darling," Ginger said as she entered the kitchen. "Ready to start this planning session?"

"I sure am." Marina took a notepad and joined her.

Marina and Ginger chose a table at the edge of the patio where Marina could see the kitchen and the entry to the cafe. If her new sous chef needed help, she was there.

Kai rushed in, wearing a glittery T-shirt with the name of a Broadway performance she had been in. "Sorry I'm late."

"I figured you might be," Marina said. "Let's get started."

Kai gave her a sideways glance. "Are you okay?"

"Why would you ask that?"

"You seem to have something on your mind," Kai replied.

Marina wasn't good at hiding her worries. She needed to talk to Heather. *Alone.* "This event, obviously." She quickly adjusted her attitude.

Ginger chuckled. "We have a lot to celebrate with this centennial."

"And we have less time than we think," Marina said. "If we work together, we can make this one of the best events Summer Beach has ever seen. The community has been good to us. I figure this is our way of giving back to the town."

Kai grinned, her strawberry blonde waves falling across her shoulders as she leaned forward. "I'm so excited. This will be an amazing show."

Ginger looked expectantly at her granddaughters. "Proper planning is key. The mayor is expecting quite a crowd, what with the promotion the city has been doing."

"Is there a theme?" Marina asked.

She hadn't been paying much attention to the centennial other than knowing it would be a busy weekend for them. Her friends at the Seabreeze Inn and the Seal Cove Inn said they had been booked for months.

Ginger looked thoughtful. "This event should honor Summer Beach's past while looking ahead to the future."

"Got it." Kai scribbled on a notepad.

Marina was still at the thinking-out-loud stage. "I like the idea of highlighting eras to create an experience that blends our rich history with our current attractions. Kai, you and Axe have built a lot of sets for the Seashell. What do you imagine?"

Kai tapped her pen. "We can organize it from the founding to today. That would make sense anyway because the glitzier floats and dance teams are in the modern era."

"That makes sense," Marina said. "With your creative director's eye, how do you envision that?"

"I'll check with people who have been building floats to see how they're representing significant eras in Summer Beach's history." Kai's enthusiasm grew as she spoke. "Like the fishermen of the early 1900s, the early surfers of the

1960s, and the town's entrepreneurs of today. It won't be a huge parade like those on television, but we can make sure it's beachy fun. That's who we are, after all."

"I love that," Marina said, warming to the idea. "Celia and Tyler have volunteered to help fund and coordinate school efforts. They're working on small floats to showcase their vision of Summer Beach's future."

"Very cool," Kai said. "We have a lot of props they can use."

"The children will love that." Ginger's eyes sparkled. "I remember the old carnivals that used to stop here. You girls always loved the Ferris wheel."

"That would be fun. Who do we call for that?" Marina asked.

"I can find out," Kai said.

"And I'll check with City Hall on permits," Marina added, making notes. Her mind already racing ahead. She looked at her list. "Now, about the classic car club."

"Nan and Arthur at Antique Times will know about that," Ginger said. "They can contact the classic car clubs. Many owners of vintage beauties would love to show them off."

Marina smiled, picturing the Main Street parade route filled with gleaming period hot rods and beach rides, engines rumbling and sunshine glittering off shiny chrome and paint.

This was beginning to take shape in her mind.

Kai drummed her fingers on the table, humming show tunes. Her eyes lit, and she snapped her fingers. "The dance studio in town competes all over Southern California. They'll have costumes and incredible routines. It will be a sparkling river of sequins and spins."

"Great idea," Marina said. "The kids would probably love to be in a parade."

"I know the owner of the dance academy," Ginger said. "I'm happy to ask her."

Kai bounced in her seat. "And we have the youth theater summer camp we're putting together this year. That would be amazing fun and exposure for them."

Her sister's enthusiasm was contagious. Ginger chuckled, and Marina pictured young dancers and aspiring Broadway stars bringing their youthful pizzazz to the parade.

Kai put a hand to her mouth. "Oh, no. Leo's friend Samantha signed up for our theater camp. I think she goes to the dance studio, too. She'll have to choose, but I'll sweeten the theater troop offering."

"I feel another rivalry developing," Ginger said, laughing.

Just then, Marina noticed Cruise hurrying toward her grandmother's cottage. "What's he doing here?"

"Who?" Kai asked, turning around.

Heather stepped out the side door and waved to him.

Marina started to get up, but Kai caught her wrist. "Relax, he's just going to see Heather. You might have fired him, but you can't fire friendship. Don't embarrass them."

Marina eased into her chair again, still chagrined at his behavior. And now, she was even more worried about Heather.

"Let's get back to work," Kai said. "What about horses? Do we know anyone who might like to ride in the parade?"

Marina thought for a moment, trying to keep her mind off Cruise and Heather. "I have a customer who invited me to her ranch. She comes into town to visit his sister. Hold on, I'll look up the number." She scrolled through her contacts on her phone. "Here she is. Jillian from Equine Rescue. Shall I call her right now?"

"Why not?" Ginger said, leaning forward. "Put her on speaker."

Marina tapped Jillian's number and waited. She recalled that Jillian said she was often out on trail rides. After a few rings, the call went through.

"Summer Beach Equine Rescue, this is Jillian speaking."

Marina introduced Kai and Ginger and told her about the centennial. "We thought some of your riders and horses might like to participate in a tribute to old Summer Beach."

"We'd love to be a part of that," Jillian said, her voice enthusiastic. "We've done this in other communities. It's wonderful exposure for our fundraising."

Marina smiled, picturing horses prancing down Main Street.

Jillian went on, "How about six riders in period costumes?"

"Perfect," Marina said. "We'll work out a good spot for you in the parade lineup to ensure the horses have a safe route and space."

She and Jillian discussed a few other details and then said their goodbyes. Marina felt a flutter of pride, knowing the parade was coming together.

Just then, she saw Heather and Cruise leaving together.

So did Kai. "Heather must be feeling better."

"She was up and out yesterday." Marina watched the two get into Cruise's convertible, her heart aching for Heather and her anger against Cruise rising.

Ginger followed her line of sight. "Do you think there might be something going on between them?"

Kai turned to Marina. "Did Heather ever tell you if she was dating anyone?"

Marina shook her head. She realized she didn't know all of Heather's friends at school. Her daughter had grown up so fast.

Kai reached for her hand. "Give her space. Heather is an adult."

"That's what I'm afraid of."

"It's hard to let a child go," Ginger said, resting her hand over Marina's.

Marina shook her head. All their lives, she'd tried to make up for Stan's death, showering the twins with attention and trying to fulfill their dreams for them. Ethan was forging ahead as young men do, but she and Heather always had a special bond. She was close to Ethan, too, but in a different way.

But clearly, something had happened.

"Come on, back to work, helicopter Mom," Kai said, tapping the table. "Let your daughter make her own mistakes. We had fun doing it. Why shouldn't she?"

Marina couldn't answer that. She looked down at her notepad.

"I might have someone we can call for a vintage surfing float," Kai said, scrolling through her phone contacts. "Duke Kalani. He was in our holiday show, *A Christmas Carol at the Beach*. That was so much fun."

Marina remembered. Duke was a local surfing legend who gave surfing lessons down the beach.

"My turn to make magic," Kai said. She tapped his name and waited for him to pick up.

"Aloha, this is Duke," a deep, friendly voice answered.

"Duke, it's Kai Moore. How's it going?"

"Kai, long time no talk. What's happening? Got another show?"

"Always, but I'm calling because of the big Summer

Beach Centennial parade. We want to showcase surfing. Thought maybe you and some friends might want to join the parade with your boards. You could help build floats. It will be so much fun, like building sets at the Seashell." She told him what she envisioned and made it seem exciting.

"Sounds epic," Duke said. "I'll spread the word."

"Totally," Kai agreed. "It will be a great party."

Kai hung up and turned to Ginger. "You're next. Who do you know who would like to be part of the centennial celebration?"

"Who doesn't she know?" Marina smiled at her grandmother.

"Well, let's see," Ginger said. "How about more music and dance?" While Kai was texting her contacts, Ginger scrolled through those on her phone and paused. "Here's one."

She put her phone on speaker in the center of the table, and the small group leaned forward as the phone rang.

"Marta, dear," Ginger said when her friend answered, exchanging pleasantries. "We're organizing a spectacular parade for the town's centennial anniversary."

"I've heard," Marta said. "And congratulations on being selected the Grand Marshall this year."

"I appreciate that, but I'd like to share the accolades. I'm sure people would be delighted if your Chorale Society would participate."

"Why, what a marvelous idea," Marta said. "I'll poll our members, but I believe the group would love to be part of this historic celebration. How about a medley of songs from the founding era through the present?"

"Wonderful," Ginger said, winking at Marina and Kai. She shared details with Marta.

After confirming the Chorale Society's involvement,

Ginger called the director of the Summer Beach Dance Academy. She proposed having the students perform chore-ographed routines as they moved along the parade route. The director readily agreed.

Ginger hung up the phone in triumph. "That's how we get things done in this town."

Kai gave her a high-five. "Way to go."

"We'll need to coordinate all the participants," Marina said as she made notes.

"Axe and I will do that," Kai said. "Staging a parade isn't that much different than staging a play. People just have to know their cues. We'll work out an order that makes sense."

They still had many details to work out, but Marina felt relieved about their progress.

Kai's phone pinged, and she quickly read a text. "More great news. I just texted my friend Theo, the juggler at the theater. He and some other street performers want to join the parade. It's a chance to showcase their talent."

"And the Seashell Amphitheater," Marina said. Kai's theatrical connections were proving valuable.

"Ooh, and I have another idea," Kai said. "Some of the makeup artists from the theater can paint faces for kids and adults. It would add to the festive spirit."

"I love it," Marina said, noting the idea. This parade would be the most colorful, lively one Summer Beach had ever seen. "Now, if only we could keep Cookie and Rosa separated. That rivalry isn't over yet."

They had both called her, angling over the prime food spots along the parade route. Even though she'd asked them to work together, old habits were hard to break.

Ginger leaned forward, steepling her fingers on the cafe

table. "I might have an idea that will satisfy them both. At the very least, it would keep them separated."

Marina and Kai looked at each other. Their grandmother's wisdom and diplomacy were legendary in Summer Beach. If anyone could broker peace between these rivals, it was Ginger.

"Here's my thought," Ginger began. "Why don't we set up two food courts, one at each end of the parade route? Cookie can have one end with her farmers market booths. Rosa can have the other end with her fish tacos and food truck friends. That way, they can divide the crowd."

Kai's face brightened. "They'd each have their own space to shine."

"Exactly," Ginger said. "There will be something—and someplace—for everyone."

"That sounds like a good plan," Marina said, quickly updating her notes. "I'll call Cookie and Rosa. With some creative scheduling, I think we can make it work smoothly."

"You always know how to bring people together," Kai said, squeezing Ginger's hand. "Or keep them apart."

Marina breathed a guarded sigh of relief. As long as they carried through with solid attention to detail, Summer Beach's centennial celebration would be on track for success. The three of them continued finalizing plans for the centennial parade, buoyed by the participation from key groups and the prospect of securing sponsorships. Jack would have his chance to add to the event as well.

With her family by her side, Marina was confident they would make this centennial celebration a success. She couldn't think of anything that might impede the flow. After all, how hard could it be to simply walk or drive along Main Street? Kai and Axe would line up people, and that would be that.

Marina checked the time, wondering when Heather would be free again. She had to speak to her soon. This wasn't a conversation she thought she would ever have with her daughter—or her son, for that matter.

But she would be brave and face the circumstances with Heather. This wasn't the worst that could happen.

Marina had brought up two children on her own. If this was the situation, they would manage. She glanced at Ginger and Kai, still happily chatting about the event planning.

After a while, Kai closed her notepad. "That's it for me today. I'll make more calls at home, but I want to put on a marinara sauce to simmer before dinner."

When Kai was gone, Marina turned to Ginger. "Do you have time to talk?"

"Of course. What's on your mind?"

Marina folded her hands to keep them from shaking. "It's about Heather."

13

*F*inally, Marina had caught up with Heather.
Ginger called when Heather arrived home, so
Marina dashed out to meet her, even though it was late.

Heather had been out late with Cruise, and yesterday,
she'd spent the entire day with Blake and the sea lion family.

Jack had wondered why Marina was going out so late.
She felt guilty about not sharing her suspicions with Jack,
but she was having a hard enough time with this herself. She
had simply told him she needed to talk to Heather.

"Come in, darling," Ginger said as she opened the door.
"Heather is upstairs in her room. Call if you need me."

"Thanks, I will. I want to talk to her alone at first."
Marina had confided in Ginger for moral support. She
didn't know how Heather would hold up through this discussion. But they would face this together as needed.

"Of course. I understand."

Marina started up the stairs, lifting one heavy foot after
the other. A cloud of anxiety settled over her. She thought of
Heather's future, dreams, and plans. The weight of this

unexpected news sagged her shoulders, and she fought to maintain her composure. In the calm world of Ginger's home, Marina was facing a potential reality that could change everything.

Ginger had helped them all through their parent's tragedy. She had continued raising Brooke and Kai, and she had been there for Marina through Stan's death and the birth of her twins. If anyone knew how to handle family situations like this, it was Ginger.

But now, it was Marina's turn. She tapped on Heather's door. "Hi honey, it's Mom. Got a minute?"

The door swung open. "What are you doing here?"

"I had to pick up something," Marina began, then shook her head. "No, that's not right. I need to talk to you."

Heather frowned and showed her in. She sat on the bed while Marina pulled a chair from the desk.

Heather was wearing a T-shirt and yoga pants. She still looked so young to Marina, but she wasn't much younger than Marina when she and Stan married.

No longer a child, but still my child. Always my baby girl.

"Did something happen with Jack?" Heather asked, wrinkling her brow with concern.

"No, he's fine."

Heather looked confused. "Then why are you here?"

Marina hardly knew where to start. An emotional weight crushed her heart, constricting her breath. Whatever had happened to her precious daughter—she blinked against a rushing range of possibilities—she had to be strong, under-standing, and empathetic.

"First of all, my darling, is there anything you want to tell me?"

"Do you mean about Blake?" Heather smiled, and her face lit. "We had the most amazing time releasing the sea lions. You should have seen them. They're so intelligent. I took videos. Here, I'll show you."

When Heather reached for her phone, Marina touched her arm. "I'm glad you got to do that, but I came here to talk about something else."

Heather drew back. "Mom, you're scaring me. Are you sick?"

"No..."

"Is it Jack? Please don't tell me you're getting a divorce."

"Nothing like that." Marina heaved a sigh. From her pocket, she brought out the test device.

"I found a box of these pregnancy tests in your bathroom. But there was one missing. Heather, sweetheart, I love you, and I am not making any judgment. But did you get a positive reading?"

Heather's eyes widened in shock, and she pressed a hand to her mouth. "Oh, my gosh, you thought that was mine?"

Marina was taken aback. "It's not?"

Heather's mouth dropped open. "What did you think?"

"That maybe you were..." Marina said, stumbling over her words.

"I'm not even seeing anyone."

"But Cruise..."

"We're friends. Well, that's all I want, anyway."

A whoosh of relief coursed through Marina. The clutter of worries and worst-case scenarios consuming her vanished. Heather's cheeks were flushed, and her eyes were bright with earnestness. In her mind, her daughter's bright future shifted back into place.

Marina held up the test device. "Whose is this?"

"Not mine, Mom. I promise." Heather's voice carried the honesty Marina knew so well.

The silence between them grew thick, interrupted only

by the rhythmic sound of the ocean. The pregnancy strip, an unwelcome element in the room just moments ago, was now merely a puzzle piece pointing to another story, another chapter in someone else's life.

Could it be Kai? The thought teased the edges of Marina's mind. Her sister had been struggling, longing for little thespians.

"Maybe Aunt Kai," Heather ventured, voicing Marina's thoughts.

"That makes sense." Marina nodded, recalling their slumber party. "She was here the other night."

Heather moved closer, her hand finding Marina's. "Maybe she didn't want to tell Axe until she was sure."

"I should talk to her," Marina said. "Tomorrow."

Inside, Marina felt her whirlwind of emotions slowing. Her mind was regaining focus. She stroked Heather's hair. "I'm glad it's not your time yet, even though we would have managed."

Heather grinned. "Me, too, Mom."

She had watched Heather grow, faced her childhood challenges with her, and dreamed of a future for her daughter unhindered by the early responsibilities of motherhood. The sudden possibility of Heather being pregnant had thrown Marina off balance.

Not because she wouldn't have supported her daughter —indeed, she would have, and with all her heart—but because she had worked and planned so that Heather could explore her young life further. She hoped her daughter could build her path without unexpected detours.

There were plenty of those in life.

"I was so scared for you," Marina said, her voice barely above a whisper. "Not because you couldn't handle it, but because I want you to have all the chances in the world. To finish college, start a career, and live your dreams without a pause."

Heather squeezed her hand. "I know, Mom. And I want those things too. But Aunt Kai? She's ready for this. Maybe it's her time."

Marina smiled, reflecting on life's unpredictability. Each path was unique. While she had prayed Heather's wouldn't include early motherhood, she fervently hoped Kai's time was now.

Marina hugged her daughter and held her, rocking slightly. Still, she was concerned about Heather out in the world, as any mother would be. "Are you being careful, honey?"

"Always, Mom."

"And you would come to me if you were in trouble? In any way, not just this scenario?"

Heather flung her arms around her. "Always," she repeated. "You're my rock, Mom. I love you."

"I love you, too, sweetheart." She tapped Heather's nose as she used to do when her daughter was young. "I hope we're celebrating with Kai soon."

Heather leaned against her. "There is something, Mom."

"Yes, honey?"

Heather smiled up at her. "I really like Blake. He'll be back this weekend. May I take some time off?"

"I insist that you do." Feeling lighter, Marina pushed off the bed and smiled. "Invite him to supper if you want. Unless you have other plans." She kissed Heather's forehead. "Goodnight, sweetheart."

Marina went downstairs, where Ginger waited for her in the living room.

Ginger looked up expectantly.

Marina shook her head. "It wasn't hers."

"Then whose?" Ginger paused. "Kai's, of course."

"It's obvious. But there was one missing."

"One that would be positive." Ginger clasped her hands. "They might be celebrating right now."

"Should we wait until she tells us?" Marina wondered. "Or tell her we know?"

Ginger pursed her lips. "Can you keep that secret?"

"Can you?" Marina asked before considering all the government secrets Ginger once had to keep. And probably still did. "I meant about this."

"Let's sleep on that, dear."

Marina hugged her before she left. On the way home, she was bursting with happiness. She opened the sunroof of her Mini Cooper and turned on her music, singing in the cool ocean breeze.

A rush of excitement surged through her. She imagined how thrilled Kai would be. She knew how much a child meant to Kai and Axe.

Why hadn't Kai told her yet? Marina wondered. Maybe Axe didn't know yet, or Kai wanted to wait a while to make sure. Now she felt guilty that Kai had missed her checkup appointment and stayed to wait tables at the cafe.

But she was so happy for Kai. Marina's heart fluttered at the thought of her sister's dreams coming true and a new addition to the family. She would respect that Kai and Axe wanted to tell everyone in their own way, but she could hardly wait to congratulate them.

Surely, Kai would share this news with them soon.

14

*B*efore the farmers market opened, Marina wove through the stalls with a rolling basket of her baked goods. Today, she had lemon-raspberry, blueberry, and apple-cinnamon muffins. She also had mushroom cheese quiche, artisan breads, and an assortment of cookies. She'd even made centennial cookies with fancy iced numerals.

Her suspicions about Kai felt heavier than the assortment of goods she was pushing. She was thrilled for Kai but wondered if she should tell Brooke. They were sisters, after all. And the news would come out sooner or later.

Brooke was already at their booth, arranging her organic vegetables in wicker baskets. She had put out green and red leaf lettuce, heirloom tomatoes, cucumbers, potted basil, and more.

"Good morning," Marina said as she began to unload her breads.

Brooke sighed and flipped her long braid over her shoulder. "If you say so."

"That doesn't sound good. Want to talk about it?" Marina noticed faint shadows under Brooke's red-rimmed eyes, the telltale signs of another sleepless night. "Did the boys keep you up again?"

Brooke rubbed her eyes. "Between sports, arguments, and all their friends, I've just about had it again. I love them all, but I need to get away sometimes. Thank goodness Chip is understanding."

"After you issued that ultimatum."

"It was for my sanity."

Marina smiled, imagining the chaos of Brooke's household. "But it worked."

She brought out the quiche and sliced one of them for samples. A lot of people grazed at the market, eating while they shopped. Others took items home. "I appreciate your waking up early for the market."

"This is my time," Brooke said. "It's when I get to have adult conversations."

If motherhood was wearing out Brooke, her pragmatic, earth-mother sister, Marina wondered how Kai would handle it. She ached to confide what she'd discovered to Brooke.

Marina tried to focus on arranging her baked goods, but her thoughts kept drifting back to Kai. *She has a glowing aura about her. Can Brooke see it, too?*

As they continued setting up, sunny morning rays chased away the chill of dawn. Around them, the chatter of vendors created a happy atmosphere. This is where Marina had started her business, and she still loved coming here.

Familiar laughter rang out, and Marina looked up.

"That sounds like Kai," Brooke said. "She's out early."

Marina chewed her lip and frowned. "She really should be getting more sleep now."

"Oh? And why would that be?" Brooke asked.

Marina put a hand to her mouth. "I didn't say anything, did I?"

"You didn't have to." A slow smile spread across her face. "I could always read you. How far along is she?"

"I haven't asked her. Actually, she doesn't know I know."

"Then how did you find out?"

Marina hesitated, searching for the right words. "Just look at her. She's like herself, but even more so."

Brooke chuckled. "Sisterly intuition only goes so far. Fess up. How did you find out?"

"I didn't tell you anything, okay? I just hope I'm right. This is such wonderful news."

"The first ones are fun, but then..." Brooke brushed away a strand of hair that had already escaped her braid. "I meant to say they're all blessings."

"Shh, here she comes," Marina whispered. "We should let her tell us."

Kai sauntered toward them, wearing a T-shirt and a short, flared skirt that showed off her toned dancer's legs. She stopped and put her hands on her hips. "You two sure shut up fast. Are you up to no good?"

Without waiting for an answer, Kai skimmed over the baked goods and vegetables. "Marina, I need at least half a dozen of your lemon-raspberry muffins for my brunch tomorrow. Plus veggies for salads, and one of those yummy centennial cookies right now."

Marina selected the muffins. "How's the renovation coming along?"

"The new bathroom is progressing," Kai replied, her face lighting up. "Being married to a contractor has its perks. You both should come by and see my enormous tub. We wanted one large enough for me and Axe."

"And are you working on any other rooms?" Marina asked.

"I'd like to add window shutters in our bedroom," Kai said.

Marina let that slide. She was referring to a baby's room, which went right past Kai.

Brooke selected some fresh cucumbers and lettuce. "For your salad. Take some tomatoes, too. You need to make sure you're getting plenty of fresh vegetables now."

"Well, sure. We all should." Kai filled her bag. "You grow the best produce at the market."

Every time Marina looked at Kai, her heart raced, debating whether to share her hunch or keep it to herself.

She looked closely at Kai for outward signs of pregnancy. Her sister looked happy and excited, and her face had a rosy glow. Unless that was her sparkly makeup. "How are you feeling, Kai?"

"Me?" Kai drew her brow. "I'm totally fine."

Brooke shot her a look. "What Marina meant was you seem awfully animated this morning."

Kai inclined her head. "That's because Jason and his wife at the candle booth just bought season tickets. I rang them up right there on my trusty little phone. I couldn't let that go."

Marina watched her closely. Kai hadn't picked up on their hints, but she was also a trained actress. She was concealing her news well. Marina should play along and act like she didn't know anything, but she could hardly stand it.

She turned to Brooke. "Should we?"

"That's up to you. You're the oldest."

Marina laughed. "You always throw that back at me when you don't want to make the decision."

Kai put a hand on her hip. "You've both been acting so strange. Would one of you let me in the secret?"

With a conspiratorial smile, Marina said, "It's your secret, Kai."

Kai tapped Marina's forehead. "Did you eat some funny mushrooms by mistake? Because you two—"

"Kai, we *know*," Marina blurted. "I saw the pregnancy kit you tried to hide in Heather's bathroom. I thought it was hers; thank goodness it wasn't."

The smile slipped from Kai's face. "Marina, this isn't funny. That wasn't mine. I'm surprised Heather would lie about that."

Her words struck Marina like a cold slap. Yet, she believed her daughter.

"She didn't lie."

Focusing on her tomatoes, Brooke averted her gaze.

And Kai was blinking back tears.

Instantly, Marina knew they'd touched a nerve. Her mind raced to the only other possibility. "Brooke?"

Her sister heaved a sigh. "We only meant to have Alder and Rowan. And then we made a mistake—but don't you ever breathe a word of that to Oakley."

"No, of course not," Marina said, putting her arm around Brooke, who had a frantic look in her eyes.

"I have no idea how I'll handle a newborn with those three wild beasts. I'm already so tired. I don't know how I'll make it. And I can't bring myself to tell Chip yet. He's already worried about their education."

"I'm happy for you, though," Kai choked out. She pressed a fist to her mouth and blinked back tears.

Marina was horrified by what she'd done. "Oh, Kai, I'm so sorry."

Kai bit her lip. "Just last week, I thought, maybe, just

maybe. And then today, wham." She smacked the back of one hand in the palm of her other.

Around them, heads swiveled at the sound.

Kai twisted her lips to one side. "No such luck, though. And Brooke just pops out babies whether she wants them or not."

This was getting out of hand. "Brooke, she didn't mean that."

"Sure she did." Brooke bit her lip. "It's true. You'd think we'd know better by now, but nothing is a hundred percent safe, except—"

"Unless you're me, of course." Kai's lips quivered, and she brushed away tears.

Brooke just shook her head. "Maybe you'll want this one, then."

Marina quickly intervened. "Brooke, please don't." This conversation was unraveling, and the market would open in a few minutes. Soon, early shoppers would flood in.

A few paces away, Ginger's voice cut through Kai's tears. "What in heaven's name is going on here?"

It was then that Marina realized other booth vendors were sending uncomfortable glances their way. "I can explain. I made an assumption, and—"

"I'm pregnant," Brooke interrupted. "But we thought Kai was, too."

"Because of the test. Of course." Ginger put her arms around Kai and Brooke, immediately grasping the situation. "Marina meant no harm, but I understand this is a sensitive subject. Kai, darling, come with me. And Brooke, we need to talk as well. Are you alright?"

Brooked nodded. "I have work to do."

Ginger steered Kai away through the stalls, and Marina turned to Brooke. "I know this is overwhelming, but I wish you'd said something. We're all here for you, Brooke."

"I suppose our family was looking forward to celebrating a new baby, but I didn't think it would be me again. And then I look at you and wonder if this could be twins. After all, it runs in the family, and with my luck..."

Marina pulled a metal bottle of water from Brooke's backpack. "Drink this. And don't even think about that. The chance is so small."

Brooke splashed her face and gulped water. "This is how couples end up with five boys."

"And every one of them a treasure," Marina said. "Any time you want to send Oakley or Rowan to my place, they'd be welcome. Leo would enjoy having someone to play with. Alder, too, although he's growing up. It won't be long before he's off on his own."

"Kids don't automatically move out these days at eighteen," Brooke said. "If this is a girl, then the three boys will have to share a room. That will start an all-out war between them. At least we had separate rooms at Ginger's. And you were away at university most of the time."

Marina recalled those days all too well. "Maybe Alder could stay with Ginger. Heather is there to help."

"That's a lot to put on Ginger. She's not as young as she used to be."

"No, but she seems to thrive with people around." Marina arranged the cookies under a glass dome as she spoke. "Can you imagine her sitting at home?"

"Maybe someday," Brooke said. "But not for a long time, I hope."

"Did she tell you that she's taking up strength training and is thinking about entering a marathon?"

"What?" Brooke's eyes widened.

"A friend of hers is a bodybuilder and has been encouraging her." Marina could hardly believe it herself.

"She should be careful," Brooke said. "I guess that's what happens when you hang around young people."

Marina laughed at that. "Actually, her friend is older than she is. She's as incredible as Ginger."

"We're half their age. Why do we feel so tired, and they're trotting around the globe?"

"Because they gave up having babies a long time ago."

Brooke looked at her and broke out laughing. "I can't believe you just said that."

"What else can we say?" Marina smiled with a small, guarded measure of relief. "Sometimes, all we can do is laugh, not that I'm minimizing your situation in any way."

"I know. Chip and I will probably find this hysterical in thirty years or so."

"I hope it won't take that long. When you're ready, let's have a celebration."

"But what about Kai…"

Marina was torn between helping Brooke embrace this pregnancy and supporting Kai in her difficulty conceiving. "We'll figure it out," she said, hugging Brooke. "We always have, and we always will."

A couple stopped at their booth, browsing the breads and vegetables.

Brooke swallowed and lifted her chin. "Looking for anything special?"

Marina was so proud of Brooke in that moment. Her sister would probably manage, but Marina wouldn't take any chances. As busy as their lives were, she would make time for family.

While Brooke helped the couple, Marina glanced toward

the edge of the market, where Ginger and Kai were talking earnestly at a small bistro table.

She and her sisters would get through this, just as they had with every adversity thrown their way. Losing their parents had forged a bond between them that nothing would break.

It occurred to Marina that this was what she wanted in her marriage. To be so sure of each other that nothing could break them and there were no secrets between them.

As Marina wrapped the bread the couple purchased, an uneasy feeling swept through her, not about Kai or Brooke, but about Jack.

She understood his professional need for discretion, but they were married now. Some things a spouse needed to know, especially if the situation might adversely impact their lives or loved ones.

While Brooke rang up the order, Marina arranged the muffins under another dome. Looking up, she saw Ginger and Kai approaching.

Brooke held out a bag to her sister. "Don't forget these."

Kai took the bag, her hand lingering on Brooke's. "I didn't mean what I said to you."

"I know." Brooke gave her an understanding smile.

"I have to go, but let's talk later," Kai said.

Ginger nodded at Brooke. "Your turn. How about a cup of tea?"

"I'd like that," Brooke replied. "Can you manage, Marina?"

"Of course." As she watched her sister leave with Ginger, Marina's thoughts returned to Jack.

When she'd been on air delivering the news, she'd had her share of threats, but that was nothing like Jack's work. His investigative work required revealing the truth, which often sent people to prison or destroyed families. That could come with a cost.

Watching Ginger put her arm around Brooke, Marina resolved to talk to Jack about his work. Honesty between them was crucial. They were married now; they were a team. While neither had much experience in long-term relationships, Marina was determined that nothing would tear them apart.

15

*J*ack carried a storage box down a wooden ladder in Ginger's garage. He and Ginger watched Leo unpack a rainbow of colorful garlands. They were planning decorations for the centennial, and she had offered anything that might be useful.

Jack chuckled at his son's enthusiasm and turned to Ginger. "You sure have a lot tucked away."

"These are from my teaching days," Ginger said, gesturing toward the neatly labeled cartons organized on shelves. "It comes in handy from time to time."

"The kids were lucky to have you for math," Jack said.

Leo looked up. "That would be cool."

Ginger smiled at the boy. "I also volunteered for drama productions, which is where Kai got her start. Imagine, a star was born right here in Summer Beach. Kai has come full circle."

"I'm going to be in the drama club this year," Leo said. "I like being on stage at the Seashell."

Ginger ruffled his hair. "Your Aunt Kai and Uncle Axe are excellent teachers. You'll have a head start in drama."

Jack glanced around the garage. This reminded him of his parent's old house in Texas. His sister was the keeper of the family history now. "This place is loaded with nostalgia."

Ginger looked up fondly. "At the time, I called it current events. Maybe I was a bit of a packrat, but at least I was well organized." She paused and pointed to another shelving unit. "That carton marked SB Photographs could prove interesting for the town's history. Would you be so kind as to bring that one down?"

"Sure." Jack started up the ladder again. He still wanted to write Ginger's biography someday. This stash of material was a goldmine he hadn't known existed. "Your garage is a researcher's dream. Why haven't we ever gone through these?"

"No need. I remember it all quite clearly."

Jack tucked the box under his arm and descended the ladder. "Do you have any interesting memories about Summer Beach for the centennial?"

"That was a hundred years ago." Leo turned to Ginger. "Were you a kid then?"

"Dear child," Ginger exclaimed. "How old do you think I am?"

Leo grinned. "Not a hundred, I guess."

"Not for many years," Ginger said. "And never forget— age is only on the outside. What's in your heart and soul never grows old."

Jack placed the dusty box on an old worktable between them. "How did you come to live in Summer Beach?"

"My parents arrived in the 1920s," she replied. "They came here for the fresh ocean breezes and the pristine beach. Around that time, a few people built summer cottages, and the Ericksons constructed their grand summer home. This cottage was Bertrand's wedding gift to me."

"Wish I could have seen it back then," Jack said, dusting off the box with a rag for her.

"I haven't seen these for years." Ginger tapped the top. "Leo, why don't you have the first look?"

The boy scrambled to his feet, lifted the lid, and peered inside. "There's all kinds of stuff in here."

"Some of it looks delicate," Jack said. A musty odor rose from the contents. "Here, I'll help you bring out this scrapbook."

Ginger smiled with recognition. "My mother created this scrapbook. Most of my photo albums are in the library or attic for safekeeping. Some of these contain extra photos, newspaper clippings, and other mementos."

"This looks pretty old." Leo sniffed.

She opened the scrapbook and sighed with pleasure. "Maybe my memory has dimmed a little. But then, it's difficult to recall every moment of one's life. Although there are people with near total recall."

Jack read the headline of an article yellowed with age mounted on a page. "Mr. and Mrs. Bertrand Delavie make their home in Summer Beach." Ginger looked about Heather's age or maybe a little older, and he could see the family resemblance.

"Wow," Leo said, looking at the clipping. "Is that really you?"

"It certainly is," Ginger replied. "I was young once, too."

As they turned the pages, Ginger's face lit at the memories. "Look, my mother included an article about the groundbreaking ceremony for City Hall."

"The town sure looks different now," Jack said.

"Everything changes, but Summer Beach has retained its charm." She turned another page. "And here is a photo of the original pier. Of course, it has been rebuilt after storms and high waves."

From between the pages, a photo of the cottage slipped out. Jack picked it up. He was enjoying going through these memories with Ginger. "The house looks brand new in this photo."

"We were just planting the property then. Look at the row of fruit trees at the rear. It would be a few years before most of them bore fruit."

"Are those the ones there now?" Leo asked.

"Most of them," Ginger replied. "Over the years, we lost a couple and added others."

On the next page was an article about a party at the cottage. "Did you do a lot of entertaining then?" he asked.

"We always loved hosting people." Ginger smiled at her recollections. "In those days, many people visited. Summer Beach was a convenient resting place, especially on narrow roads before the highway was built. We traveled at a slower place then."

"And now we have traffic to contend with," Jack said. "Doesn't help to be in a hurry." He leaned in, reading the names of people who attended the party. "How many of these people still live in Summer Beach?"

"Of those still alive, there are several," she replied. "And their descendants." She tapped one. "That is Jen's father, who started Nailed It in the village. And there is Amelia Erickson from Las Brisas del Mar."

"That's now the Seabreeze Inn," Jack said to Leo.

"This was a party to welcome newcomers to Summer Beach," Ginger said. "My parents told me the community drew many people from San Francisco looking for warmer climes. The community wasn't yet incorporated as the town of Summer Beach." She paused, smiling at her memories. "What fun we had as children, coming here every summer as the area attracted new neighbors and friends for us to play with."

Just then, Scout trotted in with a ball in his mouth and nudged Leo.

"I'll be back," Leo said, taking the ball from Scout and throwing it across the lawn. Scout took off, and Leo raced after him.

"He's a fine boy," Ginger said. "Summer Beach will be part of his legacy, too."

Curious about the photo, Jack leaned in and began to read the names printed below. "Mrs. and Mrs. John Ellsworth, Mr. and Mrs. Henri de la Fontaine, Mr. Ari Goldmann, Miss Juanita Gonzalez, Miss Pearl Park, and Mr. and Mrs. Chase Bennington." He stopped short.

"That was dear Helen and…" Ginger paused and shook her head. "She and her husband Chase were from Chicago and summered here for years. What a shame about that family. Helen was quite accomplished and intelligent."

Jack's forehead tingled. "What happened to them?"

"Fate and bad luck dogged them in every generation." Ginger shook her head. "Helen is gone now. But many called them cursed."

Were they related to the Bennington he knew? Jack had to learn more. "What do you mean by cursed?"

"While I don't believe in that, they did suffer numerous misfortunes, though some they brought on themselves." She pointed to the photo. "The elder lost everything in the 1929 stock market crash, and then they lost a child. A few years later, his parents perished on a sunken vessel off the East

Coast. While his son Chase and his family rebuilt the fortune, they employed shortcuts that weren't entirely legal. In fact, some were imprisoned for an investment scheme."

That struck a chord in Jack. "Was that recently?"

"About ten years ago. It was all over the news."

"Do you mean the Bennington Scheme?"

"Yes," Ginger replied. "Chase is serving a life sentence for it."

Surprised at the connection, Jack only nodded. *So Chaz was related. At least by marriage.*

That was years before Jack met Marina or knew of Summer Beach, so the town would have been a minor note in the article if included at all. He had investigated and written many stories in his career. He didn't recall mentioning this one to Ginger or Marina.

Even when he'd spoken to Ginger the other day, he hadn't mentioned names.

Stroking his chin, he tried to keep the curiosity out of his voice. "Wonder if any Bennington relatives still live in Summer Beach?" That might explain why Chaz visited.

"None," Ginger replied.

"How can you be so certain?"

Ginger's eyes glinted with fierceness. "There was another...situation. Chase was driven from Summer Beach."

Jack had never seen Ginger like this. "Why?"

Ginger seemed not to hear him. "It was better that they left. It's a shame what can happen to prominent families. Shirtsleeves to shirtsleeves in three generations. Deserved, of course."

He knew what she meant by part of that. Family wealth often disappeared by the third generation, with pampered grandchildren needing help understanding the drive to make money or how to steward the wealth.

But what did she mean by the *situation?* He was sure she heard him, but she chose to ignore the question. In his experience, that's where the real story was to be found. He was about to ask when he saw Marina approaching them.

"Hey, you two," Marina called out. Still wearing her chef jacket from the kitchen, she joined them in the garage. "Leo told me you were reading old newspapers in here."

"Sort of," Jack said, greeting her with a kiss on the cheek. "How's business?"

"Going well," she replied. "The new team is catching on, so I thought I'd pop over and see what you're up to."

"We've been looking through old mementos of Summer Beach," Ginger said, composing herself and motioning to the scrapbook.

Marina's eyes widened. "I've never seen any of this."

"No?" Ginger shrugged. "We've been too busy looking ahead to spend time looking back."

"Look at all this," Marina said, looking through the scrapbook. "City Hall, the pier, the old inn. Could I make copies of these to display during the centennial event?"

"What a good idea," Ginger said. "Where would you do that?"

"Maybe at City Hall, or I could enlarge some of these and place them at the cafe and other venues in town. People would enjoy learning more about the history of Summer Beach."

Admiring her ideas, Jack put his arm around Marina. "That's a great idea. Need any help with it?"

"Only if you're free."

"Almost. It wouldn't take long."

Ginger turned the page. "I will identify articles and photos of interest to the town. Many aren't."

"Did you find decorations you can use?" Marina asked.

"Sure did. Leo and I will have fun with this project." Jack had done many things in his life, but helping his son decorate an old VW van for a parade wasn't among them.

This was a new experience he would thoroughly enjoy. He wouldn't have too many more years before Leo would lose interest in a small beach town and leave to pursue his dreams.

They talked for a while, and then Marina returned to the cafe. Jack helped Ginger with a few other boxes.

As they finished, he tried posing his question again. "I had no idea Summer Beach history would read like a soap opera."

"I don't think I'd call it that," Ginger said, bristling again. "Many small towns have rivalries, bad actors, and tragedies."

"See, that's what people want to know about. The Benningtons sound like they had their share of those."

"Now, I'm not one to gossip," Ginger said, arching an eyebrow.

"This isn't gossip," Jack said quickly. "It's research. What was that situation you mentioned? Why did the Benningtons have to leave Summer Beach?"

Jack waited for her reply.

Ginger stiffened. "If you must know, it was between my Bertrand and Chase."

"Was it a financial deal that turned sour?"

"No, dear." She sighed and pressed her lips together.

"You see, I was at the center of the situation. Bertrand defended me."

Suddenly, it dawned on Jack. "Did Chase…"

"Dishonor me?" Ginger lifted her chin. "No, but he tried. Polite society didn't discuss such things back then, but I didn't let that stop me. I warned other young women."

"I bet that made you the bad guy, so to speak."

"Shocking, isn't it?" Ginger continued. "Chase had the temerity to charge that I had soiled his reputation. He had it in for us and other residents of Summer Beach."

"Sounds like it was good riddance." A thought occurred to Jack. "Where did they live?"

"On the ridgetop. They had quite a grand home, not as large as Las Brisas del Mar, but certainly overlooking it, which the owner Gustav Erickson hated. The home was sold for a pittance when property values were depressed. I don't think he ever forgave us for that."

"But he started it, right?"

She gave a sharp nod. "Chase had a way of blaming others and twisting the truth."

Jack could imagine. The man's ethics were deplorable. No wonder Chaz had chosen not to confront him. But did he carry his father-in-law's grudge? Jack could see both sides. "Who lives in the house now?"

"Carol Reston acquired the property years ago. By then, it had fallen into disrepair through several owners. She planned to restore it, but the entire structure burned before she began."

"That was a shame."

"Though not surprising." Ginger was quiet for a moment. "Chase tried to claim the property, saying it had been improperly conveyed years ago, but he lost that battle with Carol. He threatened Summer Beach officials—the whole town, in fact. He wanted the last word, and he got it."

"How?"

"By burning it down, of course. He always had a fascination with fire."

"Did he set the fire that destroyed the house?"

"Nothing could be proven. And Carol and Hal were too wise to engage with someone like that. They rebuilt, of course." Her eyes clouded again. "Chase Bennington is right where he belongs."

Jack had never heard Ginger speak like this. They had been working together for two years, and he was part of the family now, but this was beyond anything he had expected. In fact, he wondered if Marina knew about it.

Ginger heaved a sigh. "Jack, you're a talented interviewer."

"What do you mean?" he asked, feigning innocence.

"You know exactly what I mean. There are some things I seldom talk about. With good reason, as you discovered."

She closed the box firmly. "Let's highlight the positive accomplishments of the Summer Beach. We have so much to be proud of here and many talented residents to honor."

"I couldn't agree more."

He tried to shake off the feeling he had after hearing that story. The Bennington tragedy might intrigue Summer Beach residents, but he would respect Ginger's wishes.

The centennial was a time to celebrate, reflect on how far the community had come, and project into the future.

A thought occurred to him. Maybe Chaz had visited to explore his history. What else could it be?

Just then, Leo barreled toward the garage with Scout in pursuit. "Hey, Dad. Can we make a time capsule for the centennial? I read that people bury stuff to dig up a hundred years later. We can put it in our yard, but I'm not sure what to put in it."

Jack chuckled, glad that Leo had returned. "Sure, we can do that. We'll figure it out."

"Hey," Leo said, growing more excited. "Do you think there might be one from a hundred years ago around now?"

Gesturing to the wall of storage, Jack grinned. "I think we've already found it."

*a*s Jack pulled the van in front of the old citrus packing structure on the edge of town, Marina opened the window and called out to Kai, who was talking to Jen from the hardware store in the parking lot. "I didn't expect to see so many cars here."

Kai nodded. "A lot of helpers showed up."

"That's a relief. It was so good of Carol and Hal to let us use this place." Marina got out and greeted Kai with a hug.

Behind them, Jack opened the door for Ginger. Leo bounded from the back seat, eager to help carry more boxes of decorations from Ginger's garage. Jack began unloading.

Gravel crunched beneath Marina's sneakers, and pop music blasted from the warehouse. The last few weeks had flown by, and she worried they might run out of time. The committee volunteers had been working diligently to pull everything together.

A weather notification popped up on her phone as she started toward the back of the van to help. "Oh no, a tropical storm is brewing in the Pacific," she said, frowning. "It's coming up from Baja." She pressed a hand to her forehead. "And it's expected this weekend."

Kai and Ginger exchanged anxious glances. After all their hard work, would the weather ruin everything?

"Let's not panic yet," Ginger said with determination. "The forecasters will track it. Summer Beach has weathered storms before, so we'll deal with it if it comes our way. We'll postpone if we must to keep people safe."

"We never get much rain in the summer," Kai said, looking hopeful.

Marina bit her lip, thinking about their options. "The Rose Parade in Pasadena seems to carry on rain or shine, so we will, too. Unless it's a bad storm." She sighed at the thought. "I'll order clear plastic rain ponchos right away."

At the cafe, she had umbrellas covering the tables on the patio, but those were more to guard against sunshine than rain.

Kai raised her brow. "A contingency plan is always a good idea," she added, sounding uneasy. "But there's an awful lot of papier-mâché inside. That stuff doesn't like water."

Ginger squeezed both her granddaughters' hands. "No matter what happens, I'm proud of you both. You've worked so hard for this celebration. It will happen."

Marina and Kai hugged Ginger tightly. The parade plans had come together thanks to their committee and Summer Beach residents. They could only wait to see if the forces of nature would cooperate.

"What's up?" Jack asked.

Marina showed him the weather alert. "But we'll figure it out."

"You always do," he said, kissing her cheek. "That's what I love about you."

"I'll give you a hand with these." Marina picked up a box from the back of the van.

Jack shook his head. "Put it on top of this one. It's light." He carried the boxes up the ramp and Leo tagged after him.

A moment later, Jack returned, dusting his hands. "I didn't know this place existed. It's impressive."

Leo looked surprised. "Mom and I have been helping build floats here."

"Well, I've been busy wrapping up work," Jack said. "What was this old structure used for?"

"It's had a few uses, but it was built to pack citrus." Marina gazed up at the white stucco walls topped with a bell tower. "It's a Spanish Mission style of architecture."

"The surrounding property used to be a large citrus grove before Summer Beach grew in this direction," Ginger added. "Vast areas of Southern California were planted in citrus and used to supply the gold miners up north in San Francisco and the surrounding areas. Scurvy was a big problem, and people paid a lot of money for oranges back then."

"That explains how Orange County got its name," Jack said thoughtfully as he lifted another box.

"Most of that land was the old Irvine Ranch, which had hundreds of acres of citrus production." Ginger rolled back the cuffs on her pressed shirt as she spoke.

"Must have been quite the sight," Jack said.

"Imagine the scent of all those orange blossoms in the air," Marina added.

Ginger smiled at the thought. "Here, it was mostly Valencia oranges and lemons—until navel oranges arrived in Riverside County. Eliza Tibbits, a determined woman who was also an early suffragette, spearheaded that effort. In fact, her original tree still stands in Riverside. All that was before my time, but you can read more about our citrus history there." She gestured toward a historical information sign on the building. "This is a popular field trip for Summer Beach students."

"Once a teacher, always a teacher," Kai said, smiling at Ginger.

Marina pointed out the old railroad track to Leo. "You can still see the old railroad spur where crates of fruit were loaded onto the train. Be careful around those."

"Come on in," Kai said. "The floats are looking good."

"Who owns the place now?" Jack asked.

"Carol Reston and her husband," Ginger replied. "Hal housed his vintage car collection here until he sold it to raise money for charity. Now they use the space for filming."

"They also lease it for special events like the pumpkin patch and Christmas tree lots," Marina added. "We should bring Leo here in the autumn."

When they stepped inside, Marina was delighted. The entire area had been transformed into a workshop.

"This space is amazing," Jack said, taking it all in. State-of-the-art sound and lighting equipment was mounted over-head. "Imagine what you could do here."

Marina could practically see the ideas blooming in his brain. "What are you thinking of?"

"I'm not sure," he said slowly. "But this is a world-class space. Look at the systems they have in place."

"Axe used the same crew for the amphitheater," Kai said. "But right now, this a centennial wonderland."

The centennial float was outfitted with red, white, and blue garlands. Mitch's Java Beach float featured papier-mâché palm trees, a curling blue wave, and vintage beach gear.

"Wait until you see how Leilani and Roy decorate the

garden float," Kai said. "They'll bring fresh flowers and plants for it."

"It already looks charming," Marina said. The small float carried a wrought iron garden bench, gazebo, and small garden statues.

"Roy is dressing as a garden gnome, and Leilani will be a butterfly fairy." Kai grinned. "Axe and I supplied costumes."

"This will be amazing," Marina said. "Thanks for overseeing this."

"Except for loaning out costumes, we haven't done much," Kai said. "This is all volunteers, residents, and business owners."

"Who needs help?" Jack asked.

"Ask the centennial float team," Kai replied. "They've had a couple of people out sick."

Jack put his arm around Leo. "Come on, let's see if they can use the materials we brought."

"Sure, Dad."

Marina gazed after the pair, pleased that Jack had finished his portion of the article he'd been working on. His editor, Gus, had been pleased with it. However, Jack was still answering calls from former colleagues who were expanding the original scope of the story.

She wasn't entirely sure why he had backed off the story. That wasn't like Jack, but he would only say he wanted to make sure he could spend time with Leo this summer before his son returned to school. She wondered if there was another reason.

Ginger saw a friend and excused herself to chat with them.

"Do you have the parade order figured out yet?" Marina asked.

"Almost," Kai said. "We've added some latecomers, and

others have dropped out. Were you able to secure more donations?"

"Just this morning." Marina had been arranging donors for costumes for youth groups, supplies, mementos, and cleanup crews. This event was predicted to attract more tourists to Summer Beach than anticipated. "We'll have more supplies for anyone who wants to participate but needs assistance. We want all residents to feel like they're a part of the celebration."

"That's great," Kai said. "I'll make some calls."

As her sister was pulled away to render advice, Marina spied Heather on a ladder. She waved, and her daughter motioned to her. Marina made her way toward her across the warehouse.

"Hi, Mom. You remember Blake?"

The good-looking young veterinarian greeted her with a broad smile. "Nice to see you again."

"I heard you released the family of sea lions," Marina said.

Blake nodded. "I'm glad Heather got to see that. Thanks to all of you for spotting them and calling us."

"They were adorable." Heather descended the ladder, and Blake held his hand out to her.

Marina caught a look that passed between them, and she sensed a relationship developing. After the recent scare—which was Marina's fault for misreading the situation—she couldn't be happier for her daughter.

As for Kai, she wasn't talking about the subject anymore. Brooke was carrying on, and after she and Chip recovered from the initial shock, they became excited about the upcoming addition to the family.

"Blake has some wonderful news, Mom."

"About your rescue work?"

"Yes, Ma'am," he replied. "I've accepted the offer and will move to Summer Beach in two weeks."

"Why, that's wonderful," Marina exclaimed. "If you can't find anything on short notice, you're welcome to stay in our guest cottage." Since she and Jack married, they no longer needed to lease the guest room to short-term visitors.

"Thanks, I appreciate that," Blake said. "I might take you up on the offer. It's been tough to find a place in the summer."

"There will be plenty of places to choose from in the fall." Marina smiled at Heather, who looked happy over this news. They talked about Blake's new position, which sounded fascinating. And Summer Beach would be lucky to have his expertise.

"So what is this float about?" Marina asked.

"It's supposed to represent the early days of Summer Beach," Heather replied. "This structure will be one of those old-time changing rooms with striped cloth. There will be vintage bathing costumes. We found photos of a bathing beauty contest in some of Ginger's photo albums. Or rather, one that had belonged to her mother."

"That is old. And I love the idea. Who is riding on it?"

Heather and Blake exchanged another look. "We've been asked to," Heather answered. "But Ethan is bringing a golf cart to decorate. It's going to be so much fun. Would you mind? I'll work the food truck afterward."

Once in their lifetime, Marina recalled, nodding at Heather.

Her daughter beamed with excitement, and Blake put his arm around her. "I've never been in a parade before," he said. "Is this how you welcome everyone to Summer Beach?"

Marina smiled at him. "Only those who take good care of our ocean wildlife."

They all laughed, but something caught Marina's eye near another float. "Is that Cruise over there?"

Heather turned. "He's been helping out."

"Did he find another job?"

"Not yet, but he told me he has a lot of applications out."

Marina felt a twinge of guilt but stood by her decision. Being the boss wasn't easy. Not every decision was correct, but they still had to be made.

"I think he wants to talk to you."

"Heather, I hope you didn't promise him anything."

"We didn't even talk about it. But he's coming this way."

Marina sighed and turned.

Cruise hurried toward her, his sun-bleached hair brushing his shoulders. "Hey, Marina. If you have a minute, could we talk outside?"

"Cruise, I don't think——"

"Please. I just want to clear up something."

She agreed, and they walked outside.

"Do you need a reference?"

"Only if you want to give me one," he began, looking remorseful. "But what I really wanted to do was apologize. I had time to think about what I did, and I know I was wrong. You were right to fire me."

Marina hadn't expected this change of attitude. Now, she was curious. "What made you come to that conclusion?"

"I spoke to a couple of friends, and they said they would have done the same thing, only sooner." He blushed slightly. "I got ahead of myself and made a mistake with the langoustine. I will pay for the loss if you tell me how much it was. That's the least I can do."

"That's not necessary." Still, she was impressed with his offer. It restored her faith in him. She'd seen his talent from the first day, but he'd had more to learn than cooking. "I hear you've been looking for work. Any luck?"

"Not really." He tucked his chin, looking sheepish. "I don't suppose you—"

"I need someone on the food truck for the centennial. I'd like to have you back if you're not busy."

"For real?" Relief washed over his face.

"I've hired a couple of people, but I can find other venues to send you out on. How would that work for you?"

"That would be great, thank you."

"And no caviar unless the customer requests it."

"You have my word." Cruise smiled, and his entire demeanor changed.

Marina was also relieved. Even though she thought she'd made the right decision firing Cruise, she still regretted it. When she'd shared that with Jack, he'd agreed and told her a story about when he'd been in the wrong. Sometimes, people had to learn a lesson.

She had, too. She wanted to be a better manager and developer of those who worked for her. "Cruise, you're very talented. What do you want to do with your life?"

"That's easy." His face brightened. "I want to travel and cook for people around the world. Learn everything I can about how to make other types of cuisine. Everyone has to eat, and some of the best times of our lives revolve around food."

"Sort of like the chef, Anthony Bourdain?"

"He was a big inspiration to me," Cruise replied. "The food he found in his travels was incredible. Like when he discovered this incredible tasting spicy crab at a tiny restaurant under a bridge in Hong Kong."

He grew more animated, and his words tumbled out. "I've been trying to replicate that with mounds of toasted garlic and spring onions, but I don't know what the original tastes like. What I've made is delicious, but I know I can improve it. I really want to go there, and a lot of other places. Like South America, Spain, and Italy. That's just for starters."

Marina smiled at his enthusiasm. "I have a feeling you'll do all of that. I'll teach you what I can, including the business side of running a restaurant."

"I need to learn that. And a lot more."

"We never stop learning."

"I appreciate this. You won't be sorry for taking another chance on me." Cruise held out his hand.

Marina shook on their new deal. "I won't hold you back, either. When you get a better offer, and you will, you're free to leave." Working with young people, she didn't expect them to stay forever. "Ready to go back inside?"

They returned, and Marina could tell that Heather was bursting with curiosity. Ginger stood with her and Blake, admiring their work on the float.

"Let's tell them the good news," Marina suggested.

When they reached the small group, she announced that Cruise would return to work again.

"That's great," Heather said, giving him a hug.

"Congratulations," Blake added. "We haven't properly met, other than those great fish tacos you made for me a few weeks ago. I'm Blake Hayes."

"Cruise Bennington. Nice to meet you." Cruise shook his hand with gusto.

"Blake is moving to Summer Beach," Heather began.

"Excuse me," Ginger said sharply. "Did you say Bennington?"

Shifting on his feet, Cruise cast his eyes down. "Yes, ma'am."

At once, Marina felt a distinct change in the energy of their small group. What was her grandmother doing? She knew Cruise; she'd often seen him at the cafe. Yet, she had never spoken to him like this before.

Ginger pressed her lips together and lifted her chin. "Cruise, did you ever have family here in Summer Beach?"

17

*M*arina wondered what on earth was going on.

Cruise's face clouded, and he stammered for a moment. "Well, Bennington is a common name."

"Not around here," Ginger said, scrutinizing his features.

Marina touched her grandmother's hand in question, but Ginger ignored her.

Narrowing her eyes, Ginger said, "You favor someone I once knew here."

"A lot of people have an unknown doppelganger," Cruise said, averting his gaze. "If you don't mind, I have to go. I need to be somewhere else."

Marina called after him. "Come by tomorrow, and we'll devise a plan for the food truck."

Without answering, Cruise ducked out of the warehouse.

"What was that about?" Marina asked, whirling to face her grandmother.

Ginger and Jack traded a look of nervous concern. Heather picked up on it, too.

"I'll fix this," Jack said, and he hurried after Cruise.

Something wasn't right. In fact, he and Ginger barely knew Cruise, yet she had upset him with her question. Turning back to her grandmother, Marina asked, "Who did you think Cruise was related to in Summer Beach?"

Ginger shook her head, though her brow was unusually furrowed. "It was such a long time ago, dear. It's not important now."

Marina wasn't convinced. "When you say it like that, I know it is." She turned to go after Jack and Cruise, but Ginger caught her arm.

"Let Jack talk to him. He knows what happened."

"I wish I did," Marina said, holding herself back. "I hope Cruise shows up tomorrow. And I'd still like to know why he was so upset."

Ginger pressed a hand to her forehead. "I'm suddenly feeling quite weary. Ask Jack to explain everything to you, dear."

That evening, after Jack and Marina put Leo to bed, Scout loped toward them in the living room, wagging his tail and whining near the front door.

"He needs to go out for a walk," Jack said, looking for the dog's leash. "I'll take him."

"Oh, no, you don't." Marina folded her arms, unwilling to let him off that easy. "I've been waiting all evening to talk. You're not disappearing on a long walk with Scout. He can go in the backyard."

She marched to the kitchen, opened the rear door, and whistled. Scout looked confused, then bounded after her. She shut the door and returned to Jack.

"I've been waiting for your explanation," she began.

"For some reason, Ginger was emotionally spent, and you didn't want to talk in front of Leo. But I need to know what upset Cruise and why Ginger thought you could calm him down. He works for me, so this is important."

He pushed a hand through his hair. "I'm sort of caught in the middle. Did Ginger ever tell you about the Benningtons?"

"No. But why would she tell you?"

He let out a breath. "Long story. Let's sit on the front porch. I need some fresh air."

Marina couldn't imagine what was going on or how it involved Cruise. She hadn't thought her grandmother and Jack had any secrets between them.

She settled on the wooden swing they'd recently hung on the porch. "Why was Cruise so upset?"

Jack stretched his arm around her and eased the swing into a slight motion. "When we were going through her old scrapbooks in the garage, I recognized a name."

"Bennington. I don't think I've ever heard of it here in Summer Beach."

"But you have heard of it."

"Of course," Marina said, recalling how. "When I was anchoring the news in San Francisco. I reported on that financial scandal involving Charles…" She stopped. "He's still in prison. Didn't your paper break that story?"

"Yeah, that byline was one of mine. Ginger called him Chase."

"Oh, yes. I believe that's what his friends and family called him." Marina tried to recall more details, but it had happened years ago. "He dragged his son into that mess as well. As I recall, he was also incarcerated."

"His son-in-law," Jack said. "He took his wife's name when he married into the family."

It was coming back to her now. "That was considered odd at the time. Some thought he was hiding his past. But why is Ginger involved?"

Jack winced. "It's kind of personal."

"But she told you and not me?" Marina was trying to understand this, but Jack wasn't being very forthcoming,

"I got it out of her," Jack replied apologetically. "Old interviewing habits, I guess. I'm sorry."

Jack had the skill, so she understood. "Never mind, just explain this to me."

Marina listened while Jack told her everything Ginger had shared with him. A wave of sadness washed over her as she imagined Ginger, a young newlywed, having to weather that treatment.

She wished she could say times had changed more.

Yet perhaps that made Ginger stronger, forging her into the formidable woman she was today.

As they rocked on the swing in the balmy night air, Jack also told her how vindictive Chase Bennington had been about the family property. He talked about the house on the ridgetop and Chase's vendetta against Carol Reston.

"He burned the house?"

"That's what was suspected, although it was never proven," Jack replied. "I imagine Carol and Hal had attorneys who took care of that for them. They weren't living here, and Carol was touring a lot."

When he finished, Marina lifted her face to the breeze. "Now I understand why Cruise was so mortified. What a family legacy. I assume that was his father and grandfather who were convicted of fraud?"

Jack rubbed his brow. "He confirmed that today. I assured him we wouldn't spread this news around town."

"No, of course not." It wouldn't reflect well on any of

them. Still, Marina's heart clenched for the young man. "Cruise would have been young, probably about ten or twelve when his father and grandfather were removed from his life."

"That had to be pretty tough on the kid."

"I wonder if Cruise visited them in prison or kept up with them. Didn't something happen to his mother?"

"She died of a heart attack," Jack replied.

Now she remembered. "Some said it was of a broken heart. Who did Cruise live with then?"

"He was sent to boarding school."

"That's odd. He doesn't seem like the type." She smiled to herself. "Maybe that explains his affinity for caviar."

"He didn't stay but a few months. I don't know what happened to him after that."

Marina knew his resume didn't include that. As far as she could tell, he was entirely self-supporting. He worked hard, and he had his dreams. "I wonder if there is any money left in the family."

Jack shifted on the swing. "I seriously doubt it."

"Well, I'm glad you told me about this." This all made sense and put things in perspective for her. "This helps me understand Cruise better. And Ginger, of course."

He took her hand and brought it to his lip. "I hope you're not mad at me," he said, looking up at her.

With eyes too blue to be trusted, she thought, remembering her impression when they met. Why that popped into her mind, she couldn't say, but it startled her. Jack was her husband now. They shouldn't hold back.

"Are you sure you've told me everything?" she asked.

"Everything that Ginger told me."

. . .

Cruise arrived early at the cafe the following day, and Marina was pleasantly surprised. "Good to have you back, Cruise."

"Thanks for giving me another chance." A pensive look crossed his face as he tucked his hair into the band at the nape of his neck. "I guess Jack told you some stuff."

"He is my husband." Yet, Marina wasn't sure that Jack had been completely forthcoming.

Cruise picked up an apron and slid it over his T-shirt. "My dad was recently released from prison. I haven't seen him in years, and now he wants to act like nothing happened."

"Do you want to have a relationship with him?"

"I don't know the man. I hardly saw him before he went in. He worked for my grandfather, and that guy was a real piece of work."

"Sounds like no love lost there."

Cruise made a face. "Zero. He was the real criminal. My dad just went along with it. My mother told me he tried hard to win my grandfather's acceptance. But he was a harsh dude." He paused, blinking. "My mom said her father never told her he loved her."

Marina should have left it there, but Cruise seemed to need to talk about this now. "And your father did?" she asked gently.

"I don't remember, but he says he does now." He passed a hand over his stubbled jaw. "I don't have time to fix the mess he's made of his life. All I want to do is what I'm good at."

"Where did you learn to cook, Cruise?"

"Like my resume says—"

"I know what it says. But I want to hear your story."

He gave her a shy smile. "After my mother died, I was

sent to a boarding school, but I hated it. I had no friends there, and other kids stole my food. The kitchen staff saw that, so they would let me come into the kitchen and feed me. I would watch everything they did. They were my first teachers."

"Were you there long?"

"No. My uncle stopped paying for it when he found out he wouldn't be reimbursed from the estate because no money was left. I had to start earning my way. That's my origin story. You know the rest."

"Someday, you'll look back and be amazed at how much you've accomplished."

"Do you really think so?"

"I sure do," she said. "Now, let's talk about the centennial menu. We don't have much time before the event, and I want it to be fabulous."

Marina had put so much effort into the centennial—the phone calls, fundraising, and management of volunteer teams. Although she had been reticent at first, she embraced the challenge. This was her gift to Summer Beach, for supporting her in her fresh start and new life.

So many people had contributed their time. She didn't want anything to ruin this event.

18

*M*arina reviewed her centennial plan for the cafe and food truck with Cruise, and he quickly grasped what needed to be done.

"Any questions?" she asked.

Cruise grinned. "Not yet, but I'll be sure to ask this time."

"Then we'll get along just fine," Marina said, pleased with his new attitude. "While you get started, I'll check on Ginger and Heather. Be right back."

After she left him in charge of the prep work, she walked the short distance to her grandmother's cottage. Through the window, she saw Heather and Ginger having coffee. She opened the door.

Heather drained her cup and put it in the sink. "Hi, Mom. I'll shower, and then I'll see you at the cafe."

"Don't take too long," Marina said. "Today will be busy. People are in town for the centennial."

"Thank goodness Cruise is back." Heather disappeared up the stairs.

Ginger nodded toward the coffeemaker. "Fresh coffee if you want a cup."

"Just a drop." Marina poured half a cup and perched on a chair at the old red Formica and chrome table.

Ginger looked up. "Did you and Jack talk last night?"

"He told me all about what happened." She touched her grandmother's hand. "I'm sorry for what you had to go through."

"Happens all too often, but I was lucky. And I had Bertrand, who was a prince of a man."

Marina sipped her coffee, watching her grandmother. She was battle-scarred but beautiful, inside and out. "I never knew the Benningtons had a history here in Summer Beach. Why don't people talk about that?"

Ginger waved a hand. "That was so long ago. They were summer people who didn't mix with many locals. Few remain who lived here then, and even fewer knew Chase or his son Chaz."

"Cruise and I just talked," Marina said. "I told him we won't share his family's history here. His father was recently released from prison. He has been trying to reach his son, but Cruise doesn't want to talk to him. Wasn't Chaz also a victim of Chase Bennington?"

Ginger considered this. "Was he? Chaz knew what was wrong but went along with it because he enjoyed the financial benefits. That's why he was also convicted."

"Poor choices on his part then." Marina leaned forward. "Did Jack tell you he covered their story?"

"He did," Ginger replied.

"I wonder if Jack has been in touch with Cruise's father since he got out?" she ventured.

"Did you ask him?"

"He would tell me." Even as she spoke, a thought occurred to her. *If he could.*

From what Jack had told her, without discussing particulars, the story he was working on mirrored the Bennington case. Same social milieu, if different methods of fraud. Maybe Cruise's father was a source for Jack's investigations.

Ginger wasn't aware of any contact, but now Marina wasn't so sure.

Still, she wouldn't press Jack. She understood the sensitive nature of what he did and the need for confidentiality for sources.

As she walked back to the cafe, she saw the food critic Rhoda had sent. Marina called him Mr. Cufflinks; he was immaculately dressed today as well. She wondered why he had returned. And why he was heading toward the kitchen, especially since the cafe wasn't yet open.

Just then, she saw Cruise confront him. As she neared the kitchen, their conversation carried across the dining patio.

"Come with me," the older man said. "We're family."

Cruise crossed his arms. "I'm not disappearing into any government protection program with you. I have a good life here."

The man raised his hand, pointing to Cruise. "Don't talk about that."

Marina slowed her step. This man wasn't a food critic; he was Cruise's father.

Sunlight winked off a gold cufflink. "I probably won't ever see you again. And I don't know how much time I have left."

"What you've done with your life isn't my responsibility," Cruise said, smirking at him. "I'm happy right here."

"It's this town, isn't it?"

Cruise shrugged. "I like it here."

"You'd like it better if we still had our estate on the ridgetop."

"That would have been Mom's, not yours." Just then, Cruise spied her. "Look, my boss is coming. I have to go."

"Just think about it." The older man turned and strode away.

Marina exhaled the breath she realized she'd been holding and picked up her pace.

When she reached the kitchen, she put her palms on the counter. "Hey, are you okay?"

"Guess you heard that. That was my supposed father. I didn't ask him to come here."

"I know you didn't." Marina didn't mention that he'd been here before. She felt for Cruise and wanted them to get off to a good start today. "You can't choose your parents, but you can choose your life. What you were talking about earlier...do that. Follow your dreams."

"I will. And he'll be gone soon enough." Cruise flexed his jaw. "Let's just do this, can we? You said we have a million cupcakes and tons of popcorn to make."

"We sure do." She smiled and bumped his fist. They had plenty to do.

The centennial festival was almost upon them, and visitors were starting to arrive in Summer Beach. This was the most important event of the year in Summer Beach. She was invested in the event now and wanted everything they'd planned to run smoothly—the parade, food court, party, and fireworks.

Would she tell Jack about Cruise's father? No one else had seen this. At that, she turned around. Ginger's kitchen window had a clear view of the cafe's open kitchen.

As Marina cleared the counter to work, Heather arrived.

"Hey, good to see you back here," she said to Cruise. "I'll be working the food truck with you. Mom's closing the cafe during the parade so we can all go."

"Should be fun," he said. "Blake seems like a good guy. Everything okay with him?"

Heather grinned. "Stop being so protective."

"That's what guy friends are for," he said, glancing at Marina. "I look out for her. And nothing more, I promise."

"I'm glad you do," Marina said. "Although I think she manages pretty well on her own."

"But I am not making a hundred cupcakes or a ton of popcorn by myself," Heather said, and they all laughed.

Marina had created a special centennial menu for the food truck and the cafe. Simple, fun, and easy to prepare. Small slider burgers, iced cupcakes, and four flavors of popcorn: savory rosemary, sweet caramel, cheese, and white and dark chocolate.

Summer Beach was expecting thousands of visitors. Marina looked up and saw people gathering at the entry.

"Looks like the tourists are early," Marina said. "Might as well open. Let's do this." She raised her hand in a high-five, and they all slapped hands.

After lunch, Marina showed Cruise and Heather what they needed to prepare for the food truck.

"Hey, got a bowl of tortilla soup back there?" Jack called out. "I don't want to be much trouble."

"Have a seat," Marina said, giving him a kiss. The daily special was still simmering on the stove. She ladled a bowl for him and topped it with slices of avocado and cheese.

"It should be a big weekend around here." Jack sat down at the chef's table in the kitchen, and Marina placed the bowl in front of him.

When Cruise took out the trash, Marina brought Jack a

glass of water and sat beside him. "His father was here earlier. Cruise wasn't too happy about that."

"Oh?" Jack picked up his spoon.

"You haven't talked to the guy since he was released from prison, have you?"

With a soft sigh, Jack put down the spoon and took her hand. "Watch yourself around him. Please don't get involved."

She saw concern in his face and heard the worry in what he couldn't say. "I understand. Thanks for letting me know."

"There's something I've been thinking about," he said, stroking her hand as he spoke. "I've been looking for a new way to do what I'm trained to do in journalism. Something safer."

"Than illustrating children's books?" She couldn't resist.

Jack chuckled at that. "More like a forum where I could talk to people informally about their ideas. Maybe gather a few other people for casual discussion over a meal."

"That's intriguing. Talks about what?"

"Anything." Jack tapped the table as he thought. "Whatever people are good at, have discovered, or are concerned about. Did you see that kitchen at one end of the warehouse?"

Marina recalled it. "That's probably used for catering."

"People speak easier over food. Hear me out on this." Instantly, he became more excited and animated. "I've been thinking that we prepare a meal, maybe a family recipe the guest knows how to make. We could talk while we're cooking and dining. That way, it's a free-flowing, natural exchange of ideas."

It was intriguing, but... "Wait, *you're* cooking?"

"That's part of the appeal—a guy who doesn't know what he's doing."

She laughed. "That's too clichéd."

"Or…maybe I could have a chef there." He raised his brow in question.

Marina shook her head, though ideas were bubbling in her mind. "How about Cruise?"

"Not you?"

Shaking her head, she said, "You want someone young, edgy, and camera-friendly. I've done my time in front of a camera."

"Want to be my director?"

"No way. I've retired from news and media. I have a food truck empire to build now."

Jack grinned and picked up his spoon. "Sounds like we might be fighting over Cruise soon."

She looked up and saw Cruise returning to the kitchen. "He'll make his own decisions. That young man has his whole life ahead of him."

"So do we," Jack said, turning to her. "I'll call Carol and Hal this afternoon before I talk myself out of it."

"I think they'll love the idea." Feeling so proud of her husband, Marina smoothed a hand over his shoulder.

"And I promise," he added. "No more secrets between us. I mean that. My old work no longer fits into our new life."

"I'll support you in whatever you decide to do," Marina said.

Jack touched her cheek. "I need a change anyway. I want to be excited about something new, not dealing with the same old grind. I've watched you achieve your dream. Now it's my turn."

He paused and pressed his forehead to hers. "I love you, Marina. More than I ever thought possible. We'll make it through this."

"I love you, too, darling." She didn't need to ask what *this* was. "You should call Carol and Hal right after you finish that tortilla soup. Don't let either one grow cold."

He chuckled and picked up his spoon. "You really think this might work?"

Marina kissed him lightly. "I know you'll make it work."

"Just like you have," he said, brushing a strand of hair from her lashes. "First with the cafe, and now the centennial."

"Don't jinx it," she said, laughing.

"Really, what could go wrong?" he asked.

19

*J*ack threw a tattered, lime-green tennis ball on the beach, and Scout bounded after it with his slightly lopsided gait. He chuckled to himself. That was Scout's favorite toy, grimy as it was.

He turned into the morning breeze, letting it ruffle his hair as he stared across the expanse of Summer Beach. It was mostly quiet, though a few tourists were claiming their space and setting up umbrellas, chairs, and coolers. The beach would be crowded later. This was going to be the busiest weekend of the summer.

His phone shrilled in his pocket, and he pulled it out. "Jack here."

"I need to talk to you."

It was Chaz. His heart dropped. "I'm off the story."

"This isn't about that."

Scout bounded back and dropped the ball before him, panting with what looked like a big, cheesy grin.

The ocean roared in the background, making it hard to hear. "I'm busy, Chaz."

"Not that busy. Toss that ball again, then I'll meet you on the beach."

Jack closed his eyes and leaned his head back. "Where are you?"

"Turn around, my friend."

Jack hung up and threw the tennis ball. Scout took off like a rocket, spraying sand on Jack's jeans. With a sigh, he swung around. Chaz strolled toward him with a linen jacket tossed over his shoulders and polished shoes picking up wet sand.

"I would have taken you for a German Shepherd sort of man," Chaz said, extending his hand.

"Things have changed," Jack said, turning away.

"What a shame we can't be friends."

"Look, you got what you wanted. When that story breaks, it will likely put away those folks. You'll be free to do whatever you want."

"Not exactly. However, my father-in-law could use some old country club friends where he is. That's a different sort of club, of course."

"What do you want? Another media contact? Because I'm off—"

"The story. Yes, you mentioned that. Maybe there's another story right here in Summer Beach for you," Chaz said smoothly.

"I have no idea what you're talking about."

Scout trotted back, looking weary. Taking the ball, now covered in sand, he said, "Just one more time, boy."

He threw the ball again, taking out his frustration on it. Scout leapt with renewed fervor.

"Not a bad arm. Did you play ball in college?"

"Cut the small talk. What's going on?"

Chaz turned toward the Coral Cafe. "You're a smart

man. What with the community's quaint historical celebration, I suspect you might have uncovered my family's
history."

Uncomfortable, Jack followed his gaze. "Your wife's
family, that is."

The other man sniffed at that. "When I married, the
Benningtons became my family for obvious reasons. I never
thought I would see that in print. Or answer questions about
my past in a courtroom. You have no idea how difficult that
was."

"More difficult than facing the families your company
had financially ruined?"

He shrugged. "People should be more careful."

"Even after all this time, you show little remorse for
those you defrauded. If you had, you might have gotten off
with probation."

"I did nothing of the sort. My father-in-law——"

"What is it, Chaz?" Jack gritted his teeth, every second
an eternity with this man.

The other man lifted his chin. "You have doubtlessly
ascertained my relationship with your wife's young chef."

"I have."

"This town ruined my family." He raised a hand,
pointing toward Carol Reston's home on the ridge. "That
was our estate. It should still be ours."

A strange sense of warning tickled Jack's neck. "You're
living in the past. Let it go."

"I will not let the small-minded people of this town ruin
my son, too."

Jack knew he should have walked away when Chaz
approached him. But now it was too late. "I'm not following
you."

"Cruise refuses to leave." Chaz scoffed at the thought.

"After this trial, and I share what I know, he could live with me anywhere in the world in a witness protection program. We would be protected by the very people who sought to destroy me. Delicious, isn't it?"

A chill ran along Jack's spine. "You can't make Cruise go with you. What if the townspeople share the Bennington history with him and turn him against you? How will his grandfather feel about that?"

Chaz flexed his jaw, and his eyes glazed over. "The spiteful people of Summer Beach will never forget me or the Benningtons. My father-in-law will appreciate my actions, mark my words. He should have been the Grand Marshal, not *her*. Ginger Delavie ruined our family. But what I plan to do will go down in history."

Scout raced through the surf, splashing Chaz's polished shoes and shocking him from his vindictive trance.

Chaz sputtered, "You'll see soon enough."

"See what?" Jack was grasping for any information he might spill.

Chaz waved him away and charged off across the sand.

While Jack watched the broken, bitter man stumble and slip on the sand in his misplaced anger, Scout whined by his feet.

"That's it for today, old boy." Jack rinsed off the ball and pocketed it.

Still, Scout whined after Chaz.

It occurred to Jack that even the dog knew something was wrong with that character. "Come on, boy. We need to see Ginger right away." Urgency gripped him, and he hurried toward the coral-colored cottage.

Jack stepped onto the front porch. "Wait here with those sandy paws," he said to Scout, who obediently flopped down. As he wiped his feet on the mat, he tried the front doorknob and pushed the door open. "Is everyone decent?"

"Why, come in," Ginger said. "We're in the kitchen putting more muffins in the oven."

When he strode into the kitchen, Marina looked up in surprise. "I thought you were picking up Leo this morning."

"Something came up. That door needs to be kept locked," he added, sharper than he'd intended, but his heart was racing. He needed to check on Leo, too. "There are all kinds of people out there, especially this weekend."

Marina's mouth opened. "What happened?"

"Chaz found me on the beach." Running a hand through his hair, Jack paused to compose himself. "He's planning something, and he was baiting me. I don't know what he's going to do, but we must stop him."

Ginger raised herself up, steeling her gaze. "That vengeful little man. I am not surprised. So like his father."

"We have to call Chief Clarkson," Marina said. "And I'll tell Cruise."

"I'll warn Vanessa," Jack said, trying to calm his breathing. "And someone should call Carol Reston."

"I'll do that," Ginger said. "She is performing tomorrow."

Jack had a sickening feeling about this. "She's the surprise guest? Marina, why didn't you tell me?"

She turned up her palms. "I figured you knew after you called them about the warehouse. And it was meant to be a surprise."

Jack pressed a hand to his forehead. The conversation with Carol and Hal had gone as well as he had hoped, but they didn't discuss the centennial.

"Who is calling the chief of police?" Ginger asked.

Marina pulled her phone from her pocket. "I'll put him on speaker."

Just then, Heather came downstairs. "Mom, what's going on?"

Marina shot Jack a look. "Honey, go get Cruise and bring him back here. We'll fill you in together."

"Okay, whatever." Heather looked confused, but she started toward the cafe.

"No, wait," Jack said, touching her shoulder. "Text him and tell him to come in here. No one leaves right now."

"It's Cruise's father," Marina said. "He's threatening the town. Maybe this weekend."

Heather looked between them all. "Not the centennial," she said, clearly dismayed.

Marina hugged her, and Jack put his arms around them. Marina's heart was beating as fast as his. "I'm so sorry, but we'll stop him."

Guilt threatened to overwhelm him. They wouldn't be in this situation if he hadn't pitched that story and opened a portal to the past.

He punched in a quick text to Vanessa about Leo. "Let's make that call."

"Is something burning?" Heather asked, sniffing the air.

"Oh dear," Ginger said. "The cupcakes."

"I got it," Cruise said, bounding into the kitchen. Grabbing a dishtowel, he opened the oven. He pulled out a tray of burned muffins before facing everyone. "What's going on?"

"Breakfast is delayed, I'm afraid," Marina said. "It's about your father."

"I don't have a father," Cruise growled.

"Hang onto that thought," Jack said, placing his phone

on the red kitchen table. He dialed and turned on the speaker.

When Chief Clark answered, Jack quickly told him the background of what was going on. "Chaz Bennington has issued a threat against Summer Beach. I think he'll try something at the centennial celebration."

Turmoil churned within him. The event that everyone had worked so hard on should be a time of unity and reflection, but now it was marred by a threat.

There was a brief pause on the other end. "Jack, you're sure about this?" Chief Clarkson's voice was always steady. It was one of the reasons Jack respected him so much.

"I wouldn't raise the alarm if I wasn't." Jack told Clark what he knew. "We're all with Ginger at the Coral Cottage."

"Alright," Chief Clarkson replied. "We'll take it from here. You were right to call, Jack. Keep them safe."

Jack's heart raced, his protective instincts firing. "I'll do that. But I can't just sit this out. I can be there in five minutes."

"You've done your part, so let us handle this. I'll send a patrol car to the cottage. Do you have any idea where this guy might be?"

Jack turned to Cruise, who shook his head. "None of us know." He hung up, feeling the heavy weight of responsibility for this situation.

Angered, Cruise punched the air. "That man can burn for all I care."

"Interesting choice of words," Jack said. Suddenly, he had an idea. He called up the number for Nailed It. Jen answered.

"Hi Jen, it's Jack. I was wondering if you carry gas cans."

"Sure do," came her reply. "Want me to put the last one aside for you?"

"The last one?" he intoned, feeling sick.

"Some guy bought several yesterday, but we had one in the back stock that I found and just put out."

Jack rose from the table. "Don't sell it. I'll explain later. Chief Clarkson might be calling you." With his stomach twisting, he hung up.

Marina gathered Heather and Ginger in her arms. "We need to watch the house right now."

"And the cafe," Ginger added with a look of determination.

Cruise clenched his jaw, and everyone nodded. Jack turned to Cruise. "You and I need to guard the property. Are you up for it?"

The younger man nodded. "Chaz won't get away with this."

Shivering with concern, Heather threw her arms around Cruise's neck. "Be careful out there."

Smiling at her, Cruise kissed the top of her head. "I'd never let anything happen to you."

Jack's mind raced. Had he done enough, and would Chief Clarkson locate Chaz in time?

After all this, he hoped the heart and spirit of Summer Beach would shine through, undimmed by the dark soul who sought to destroy it.

20

*T*hin morning rays filtered through the window, waking Marina. Immediately, she checked the weather forecast on her phone and breathed in relief. She lifted herself on one arm and shook Jack, who was barely awake.

"Listen to this," she said. "The storm veered off into the Pacific and dissipated. We have clear skies today for the centennial."

Jack rolled over in bed and hugged her. "My wife is incredible. She even controls the weather."

Laughing, she thumped his bare chest. "Come on, we have a big day ahead of us. I'm so excited."

He framed her face in his hands. "And I need to check in with Chief Clarkson about the Chaz issue."

At the sound of that name, Marina blinked, the memory of yesterday casting a cloud over what should be a sunny day. "Check your phone."

They had taken turns watching Ginger's property yesterday until the Summer Beach police parked a cruiser there. Marina opened the cafe, and it soon was packed with customers as people poured in for the weekend festivities. Heather, Cruise, and the new staff had worked late preparing food and loading the food truck for today.

Still, they were all concerned about what Chaz might have planned. Chief Clarkson promised to let them know when he was located.

Jack reached for his phone to check on the news and frowned. "No word yet. I'm sorry if this puts a damper on the celebration."

"It's not your fault," she said, threading her fingers through his thick, unruly hair. "How could you have known he would make such a threat? But I refuse to let him spoil this event."

"That's the spirit." Jack smiled with encouragement and pressed his lips to hers. "When he makes his appearance, we'll be ready for him. Clark and his police force are poised to act."

Marina had to trust that. "We can't let one man's attitude derail all the work volunteers have put into this day of celebration." Still, she was uncomfortably aware of the risk.

Jack smoothed her hair from her forehead. "I promise I'm leaving this kind of work behind. I can't put you or Leo at risk anymore. Believe me, plenty of young, hungry writers will be thrilled to get my story assignments. I've already told Gus, and this only reinforces my commitment. I have other options."

She was relieved to know that. "I'm sure we'll hear from Clark soon." She was worried, but she was trying not to let it show. Jack felt bad enough.

Yesterday, Chief Clarkson told them he had arranged for off-duty police officers from neighboring communities to help with the crowd and anything that might happen.

Marina sent a message out to all volunteers, asking that if they saw any questionable people or unusual behavior, they should immediately contact the police. That was a good practice anyway, she told herself.

She pushed herself up from the bed, but Jack wrapped his arms around her before she could leave. "Hey, aren't you forgetting something?" he growled.

"I don't think so," she said, smiling down at him. "We have to hurry, Jack."

"We have a couple of minutes." He started laughing. "At least enough time to wish you a happy anniversary, darling."

Marina laughed with him. "Oh, my goodness, so it is."

"I bet you thought I would forget." He clasped her hands and kissed them. "We can have a personal celebration later." He waggled his eyebrows. "What do you say to next weekend at Beaches—just you, me, and Scout?"

She laughed at what had now become a joke between them. "How about next weekend anywhere else?"

"You're on." He pulled her up, twirled her around, and swayed with her from the bedroom, his hands spanning her waist.

While Jack woke Leo, Marina made protein shakes blended with spinach and fruit to tide them over.

They had planned that Jack and Leo would decorate the van while Marina and her team finished loading the food truck. Denise and John were bringing Samantha, who would also help decorate with Leo. Marina drove her car to check on the festival venue and Kai at the warehouse.

When they arrived, the scent of popcorn filled the air. Heather bounded outside to greet them. She was already dressed, with her long hair clasped into a ponytail.

"You're ready early," Marina said, hugging her. "I thought I'd have to wake you."

"Cruise called me at sunrise. He's been popping corn since daybreak." Heather's eyes widened. "Oh, my gosh, your recipe for popcorn drizzled with white and dark chocolate is amazing. I had that for breakfast."

Marina laughed. "I'm glad you liked that but eat something healthy. You'll need your strength today." She glanced at the food truck.

Cruise saw her through the window and waved.

"How is he doing?" Marina noticed that he and Heather had been talking a lot yesterday.

Heather quirked her mouth to one side. "He's a good guy, so he's awfully upset about his dad. I can't imagine having someone like that for a father. He's sort of envious of me for never having known my dad."

"I wish you had," Marina said, touching Heather's shoulder. "He was one of the good ones. When is Ethan coming?"

"Soon. He's bringing a golf cart to cruise in the parade. Blake and I will join him, and then I'll help Cruise on the food truck afterward."

"If you're not needed, you can take off this afternoon," Marina said. "We have more help now."

"Thanks, Mom. I really want Ethan to meet Blake. If we're swamped on the food truck, I figured they could entertain each other. Or Blake could help Cruise on popcorn duty."

Marina smiled. "I think Blake would rather spend time with you. He seems pretty taken with you."

Heather's face colored slightly. "I feel the same way about him. He's so smart, we can talk for hours. He loves Summer Beach, too."

"That's a big plus," Marina said. She didn't want to push her daughter in any direction she didn't like, but she would love to have her nearby.

Ginger appeared on the steps of her cottage with a basket over her arm. She waved to them before walking to the patrol car parked in front of her house. Marina watched to see what she was up to, but she had a pretty good idea.

"Good morning, officers," Ginger said. "I brought you some muffins and quiche fresh from the oven. We appreciate you keeping an eye on us."

The officers thanked her profusely.

Satisfied, Ginger joined Marina and Jack. "Keeping the officers sharp is important," she said, hugging her daughter.

"We appreciate that, too." Marina looked at her watch. "I need to check on the Main Street venue to make sure everything is set up there. Some volunteers are already there. Then, I want to see Kai to ensure everything is on schedule with the parade. It won't take long."

"Let's go," Jack said.

"You can stay here with Leo to decorate the van together," Marina said. "I have my car."

A concerned expression clouded his face. "I'd feel better going with you."

Ginger pressed a hand on Jack's shoulder. "Why don't you two go? I'll keep Leo company."

"He's probably hungry," Marina said. "We didn't have time for much this morning. Samantha and her family will be here soon, too." Feeling slightly concerned, she glanced around the property, her gaze settling on the police car.

"I have another quiche and muffins in the kitchen," Ginger said. "No one here will starve."

Satisfied that everything was under control, Marina and Jack set off.

"Want me to drive?" Jack asked.

"Sure." Marina tossed him the keys, and he opened the door for her.

They drove the short distance to Main Street and parked. Volunteers were setting up folding chairs in an easily accessible section reserved for those with mobility issues. Many people would bring camp chairs to watch the parade.

Ginger's vintage photos that Jack had enlarged were displayed in the old section of Main Street and in some shop windows. Early morning walkers were stopping to read the captions Jack had added, clearly intrigued.

"That was a good idea," Marina said. "The history of Summer Beach is fascinating. Those photos really bring it to life."

Walking around the bustling food area, they saw vendors setting up booths and food trucks arriving. They passed stalls with names etched in wood and painted in bright colors.

"Here's Cookie's stall," Marina said, admiring her friend's artistry with pastries.

Cookie's Confections was a colorful palette of decadent strawberry tarts, lemon cookies, and blueberry turnovers.

Next to her was Rosa's Tacos, where Rosa's husband tended the grill in the food truck parked behind them for fish tacos. Rosa was arranging containers of homemade guacamole, spicy salsa, and crispy tortilla chips on the table.

Jack raised his brow. "Seems odd that Rosa is right beside her."

Yet, there they were. Two former rivals, Rosa and Cookie, talking and laughing like old friends.

Marina was amazed. "Are you seeing this?" she whispered to Jack.

He chuckled. "Seems like they've finally made up.

Making them work together was brilliant. Guess that means no food fights at the event, though. That part of the entertainment will be sorely missed."

After talking to Rosa and Cookie, they continued to check on the parade route and the podium area for speeches. While they walked the area, they both kept an eye out for Chaz. Jack was convinced he would make a move today, though Marina still hoped it was simply boastful talk.

Jack paused at the entrance to a small carnival with rides already set up near the pier. "Leo and Samantha will want to come here."

The major attractions were a Ferris wheel, a merry-go-round, a fun house, and games of chance. Stuffed animal prizes hung from tall poles, and spun sugar cotton candy smelled sweetly intoxicating.

"Everything is coming together," Marina said, excited and relieved. "Let's see how Kai and Axe are doing at the warehouse."

They got into the Mini Cooper. Before starting the car, Jack glanced at the fuel gauge. "We should stop for gas on the way."

"This gets better mileage than the van. I'm sure we can make it."

Jack raised his brow. "How would that look if we ran out of gas on the way to the parade? We have time to fill the tank. Besides, I don't like to see you driving a car so low on fuel."

"I love you, too," she said, kissing his cheek. "There's a convenience store with gas pumps not far from here."

This was one of the thoughtful acts Jack did for her, and she appreciated it more than he knew. Taking care of small things for each other was one way they showed their love.

After a few minutes, Jack pulled into the convenience

store parking lot and alongside a bank of gas pumps. Traffic into Summer Beach for the centennial was beginning to build, but they could take shortcuts back.

Jack stepped from the car, swiped his credit card, and put the nozzle into the tank. As the car filled with gas, he slid back into the seat, leaving the door slightly ajar. "Need a coffee from inside?"

"Sure, that sounds—" When Marina turned to him, a chill shot through her, and she froze. "Don't look behind you. Chaz just pulled up in a car on the other side of the pumps."

"No problem, I'll deal with him," Jack said, starting to get out.

"No, don't," Marina whispered, grabbing his wrist. "If he's planning something, he might be armed. We can't leave."

Surreptitiously, she slid out her phone. "I'll call the police."

"Don't hold up your phone," Jack said quietly.

Keeping an eye on Chaz, Marina opened her purse and brought out another small white case. She extracted one earbud. After placing it in her ear, she tapped an emergency number on the phone in her lap.

As it rang, she said softly, "He just pulled three gas cans from the trunk."

"Hurry," Jack breathed.

The dispatch answered.

"Can you hear me?" Marina asked in a barely audible whisper. When the dispatcher confirmed, she quickly gave her name and location. "We've just spotted Chaz Bennington. We're filling the car with gas." She answered a few questions, and the dispatcher instructed her to stay on the phone.

"Don't turn away from me," Marina said, holding Jack's gaze. Every muscle in his face and body was tense. The smell of gas infiltrated the car, making her slightly nauseous.

A movement in the rearview mirror caught Jack's eye. "He's walking behind us. Going into the station. Don't move because he can see through the windows."

Marina held as still as she could. She didn't think Chaz knew her car.

After an eternity, he emerged from the store, counting his change and stuffing a handful of lighters into his jacket pocket.

"Tell them to please hurry," Marina whispered, relaying what she saw to the dispatcher.

Watching in the rearview mirror, she saw a police car turning in. The dispatcher continued speaking to her.

However, instead of walking behind the car, Chaz cut in front. As he did, he looked up, squinting into the sun.

Suddenly, he scowled and started toward them.

"Get down," Jack cried in a hoarse whisper. "He saw us."

Chaz quickened his steps toward the driver's side.

"Let's get out of here," Marina cried. She slid to the floor, curling into the tight space.

"Hold on." Jack started the engine, preparing to leave, even with the gas nozzle and hose still attached.

Just then, a siren blasted, a police cruiser pulled in front of Chaz's car, and another hemmed him in from the rear.

Doors slammed, and Marina could hear the officers addressing Chaz. Shaking, she pulled Jack down with her.

He threw his arms around her, shielding her with his body and clutching her with such strength that she could barely breathe.

"Stay calm, ma'am," the dispatcher said.

Despite her heart pounding, Marina could hear the commotion outside growing louder. She prayed Chaz would give himself up; she worried he might be tempted to make a scene. He had so little to lose now.

However, after a few tense minutes, Chaz surrendered.

At last, the dispatcher released her, and she hung up the phone, flooded with relief. "Thank heavens," she said, pressing her hands to her throbbing temples.

Jack stepped from the car to remove the gas nozzle, and Marina hoisted herself back into her seat. When a tall, barrel-chested officer approached the car, she cried out, so happy to see their friend Clark.

"Chief Clarkson," Jack said, clasping his hand. "It sure is good to see you."

"You two were fortunate," Clark said, jerking a thumb toward the other squad car where Chaz had been placed and secured. "And you likely saved the town from a potential disaster. Before I let you go, I need details for the record."

After giving their statements, Marina felt drained. Even her hands tingled, and she was slightly dizzy from the stress.

She reached for Jack and rested her head on his shoulder. "Having worked on the front lines in news coverage, you're probably used to this, but I'm a wreck."

"I was a lot younger then, and I didn't have any responsibilities," Jack said with a distant look in his eyes. "I'm rattled, too. I kept thinking of you, Leo, and our families. This day could have taken a horrific turn for the worse. Thank goodness your gas tank was nearly empty."

Although the morning chill was burning off, Marina shivered. "Is your offer for coffee still good?"

"You bet it is." Jack slid his arms around her and kissed her. "Come with me inside, though. I can't leave you alone, not after that."

"I'm so thankful we were together," she said, clutching his arm. "If I'd seen him on my own…"

"You would have done exactly what you did," he said, tilting her chin for a soft kiss. "I know you, and I admire your grace under pressure. There is no one I'd rather have by my side in any situation. You're my wife, my partner, my everything. This is one anniversary we won't forget."

The tears Marina had held back filled her eyes, and she choked on a sob. "I love you so much. That could have ended terribly… I don't even want to think about it."

"Don't," he said, rocking her in his arms. "That's a rare occurrence in Summer Beach."

Marina noticed his chest quivering and realized he was shaking, too. She knew this was a normal physical response after a tense flight or fight situation.

She kissed him and pulled back. "Shake your hands as hard as you can with me. Ginger once told me it helps release muscular tension and calm the nervous system."

He grinned, and they shook out the stress they'd just endured.

"Feel better?" she asked, slightly winded.

"Actually, that helped." He let out a chuckle. "Let's get that cuppa brew now."

They walked into the convenience store for coffee and then returned to the car. They sat for a few minutes, calling their loved ones with the news and composing themselves for the day ahead. Kai was shocked, and Axe wanted to rescue them, but Marina and Jack assured them they were okay and would see them shortly.

After hanging up the phone, Jack reached for her. "Ready for that celebration?" he asked, massaging her neck.

"In so many ways," she replied.

21

*W*hen Marina and Jack arrived at the warehouse, the entire facility buzzed with volunteers preparing for the parade. All around them, people were laughing and lining up, getting ready to go to Main Street.

The news of Chaz's arrest had spread among them as well. When people saw them, they applauded and called out to them.

"Way to go, Jack," Axe said, and everyone laughed.

Kai greeted them both with hugs. "Oh, my gosh, I was so worried about you. Are you okay?"

"It's over, and we're ready to celebrate," Marina said, clasping her sister's hands. "I am so relieved to see you."

"You're such a rock star," Kai said, her eyes glistening with the emotional release. "Both of you are like super-heroes, saving the town from an evil antagonist."

Marina laughed. "And you've been watching too many movies." But she loved Kai's enthusiasm. Her sister always spoke from the heart.

Axe threw his arms around Marina and Jack in a huge embrace. "Glad you two made it through that situation," he said. "We have a lot to celebrate today, including that."

"And it looks like everyone is ready," Marina said, looking around in awe at the colorful riot of creativity.

Kai clutched a clipboard to her chest. "What do you think of everyone's efforts?"

"All the floats turned out so well," Marina replied, surprised at the artistry and imagination on display. "I would have never imagined all this. Here's to the parade directors."

"Our pleasure." Kai took a little bow in her vintage-inspired beach outfit. She wore a bright floral halter top and a wraparound skirt. Axe wore a matching shirt and board shorts.

Kai lowered her voice, her eyes glittering with excitement. "We're performing our beach medley on a float, and Carol Reston will join us for the final number at the end as a surprise. No one knows."

"Everyone will love that." Marina was so moved by all the work put into the event.

Her heart swelled at the array of floats, each a testament to the rich tapestry of Summer Beach's history. She pressed a hand to her chest, suddenly overcome by the happy spectacle. Her emotions were still raw.

"It's so much more than I expected, too." Jack's hand found hers, and he gave it a gentle squeeze.

The incident that threatened to overshadow the day was now a memory, dispersed like the morning mist. Marina drew a steadying breath while she watched the bustle and commotion around them.

Many of their friends were putting the finishing touches on their floats. Others were securing their flatbed trailers to vehicles, primarily SUVs and pickup trucks that had been decorated, too.

Jen and George from Nailed It were helping people with last-minute repairs. Jen looked up and waved; she pressed a hand to her heart. *Thank you*, she mouthed.

Marina waved back, grateful for Jen's friendship. The news had traveled fast.

Leilani and Roy's Hidden Garden float bloomed with a stunning variety of potted plants and flowers. Pink bougainvillea arched over a white gazebo, and yellow roses flanked a garden bench. The couple were in costumes, with Leilani dressed as a garden fairy.

Kai clapped her hands. She was a force of nature, her voice clear and confident as she directed volunteers with the efficiency of a seasoned director.

"Remember, we're not just celebrating a centennial; we're telling a story of the birth of our community," Kai said, scanning the floats.

Standing beside her, Axe nodded in agreement, his baritone voice carrying through the warehouse. "We need everyone to line up in the order posted. Where you're ready, we'll lead the way to Main Street."

"Once there, we'll include others," Kai said. "The equestrians with their prancing horses, the school marching band, and the dance teams."

Jack took Marina's hand and squeezed it. "Best parade ever."

"Thanks to Kai and Axe," she said.

"And your leadership." Jack kissed her on the cheek. "You managed to rally volunteers and obtain donations. Without you, this would have been sheer chaos."

"I appreciate that," Marina said, grateful for everyone's efforts. "So many people contributed."

Marina admired the floats that were now lining up, snaking around the perimeter of the warehouse. The Founders float boasted miniature cottages and a sandy beach, while the surfing float featured vintage boards. Duke stood at the center of it, waving, with Mitch right behind on the Java Beach float. The Summer Beach Art Guild float held easels with local works, portraying a community that encouraged and supported creativity.

Axe blew a whistle that hung around his neck. "When I give the signal, we'll take off. Everyone should stay in line and take it slow."

"This will take a while," Kai said, grinning. "We'll have a police escort because we'll be holding up traffic."

Marina gave her sister a hug. "We'll see you soon on the other side."

They were running late now, but Marina had also allowed ample time before the event, just in case.

By the time Marina and Jack returned to the Coral Cottage, Cruise and the new team had completed loading and organizing the food truck.

Blake had arrived, and he had pitched in with Heather. Marina saw a happy spark in Heather's eyes. Blake looked like he was enjoying himself, too.

After Marina approved what they had loaded on board, Cruise started the truck. He and the team took off to meet Rosa and Cookie in the food court area. Heather and Blake stayed behind to wait for Ethan.

Leo and Samantha were finishing their decorating. "What do you think, Dad?"

"Best this van has ever looked," Jack said, high-fiving them.

With John and Denise's help, the kids had lashed an old surfboard Ginger had in the garage to the top and laced bright garlands around the windows. They had drawn an enormous birthday cake with 100 candles on a roll of white butcher paper and taped it to the van. It read, *Happy Birthday Summer Beach.*

"Miss Ginger said I can ride in the Mayor's car, too," Samantha said, hopping from one foot to another in excitement.

Ginger hugged the two children to her side. "I'm thrilled to have my two bright sidekicks with me. I couldn't be more pleased."

"Thank you, Ginger," Jack said with a hand to his heart. "This means so much to the kids."

Marina took a few photos of Ginger with the children and their handiwork, wanting to remember everything about this special day.

A few minutes later, the mayor arrived with his wife Ivy, owner of the Seabreeze Inn. They drove Ivy's cherry red 1950s Chevy convertible with the top down, waving as they pulled to the curb.

Bennett and Ivy stepped out of the car. "We're here for our esteemed Grand Marshal to lead the parade," he said, greeting Ginger.

After discussing logistics, Bennett took the wheel with Ivy beside him. Behind them, Ginger sat on a red leather bench seat like an empress, her head held high and a confident smile wreathing her lovely face. Leo and Samantha scrambled into the convertible on either side of her, beaming with excitement.

"Better practice your wave," Marina said to them, laughing and waving goodbye. "See you there soon."

As they were leaving, Ethan arrived, towing a golf cart he and his friends had started decorating. "Hey, Heather. Blake, good to see you. I've heard a lot about you."

Blake grasped Ethan's hand. "Likewise. Thanks for including me."

Marina watched as the three of them unloaded the golf cart. She helped Heather hang fluffy pom-pom decorations on the roof of the cart. With a few finishing touches, the kids climbed in. Ethan and Blake were already chatting easily and trading jokes.

Ethan put on a cap. "I'm your golf cart chauffeur. At your service." They all laughed.

"See you there," Heather said, happily snuggling beside Blake in the rear seat.

"There they go," Marina said, wistful at seeing Heather take off with Blake and her brother. "It seems like they grew up overnight."

"I suppose Leo will do the same thing." Jack put his arm around her. "Ethan and Blake seem to have hit it off. That's a good sign, isn't it?"

"It is," Marina agreed, understanding how essential it was to the twins that the other accepted the person they were dating. That hadn't always been the case. For Heather's sake, she hoped the two men would get along.

They walked toward the van, chuckling over how the kids had decorated it.

"Leo is thrilled that we're in the parade, too," Marina said, sliding her hand through a crook in Jack's arm. "This will be fun."

"You've done a good job of coordinating everyone. You're pretty impressive, and I'm not saying that just because we're married."

Marina laughed, but she accepted his praise. Her teams of volunteers handled their respective tasks well, so she felt good about the entire event. After the stressful event of the morning, she was beginning to relax.

As they neared the starting point for the parade, Marina glimpsed the sun glinting off the ocean. Not a cloud sky, she noted, pleased. They would have no use for the plastic rain ponchos she's ordered, although they would come in handy during the rainy season.

"It's going to be a wonderful day after all," she said to Jack, who squeezed her hand in response.

They were only minutes from Main Street. Once they arrived, Kai and Axe were busy confirming the order of the parade participants and adding new ones to the lineup.

Axe blew his whistle, getting everyone's attention.

"The bike brigade should be right here," Kai said, indicating a spot in the line. "If you're riding a bike, join me here." Several children fell in line, their bikes festooned with streamers and balloons, and their faces alight with excitement.

"Where do you want us?" Marina asked.

Kai motioned to a place behind the Java Beach float. "Right there is perfect; you all have the vintage beach vibe going. Did you see how many people are lining Main Street? I've never seen so many visitors in town."

"That's fantastic for the shopkeepers on Main," Marina said.

Kai nodded, glancing at her watch. "Are you opening the cafe after the parade?"

"We'll be open for dinner. People want to see the fireworks from the dining patio. I'm sure we'll be busy."

"Not everyone can live on hot dogs and cotton candy," Kai said. "Tempting as it might be."

Marina and Jack climbed into the van and pulled behind Duke. They were in the middle of the procession.

Axe blew his whistle again. "Now that you're lined up, stay in that order. Kai and I need to jump on our platform for our musical number. Taking our place here is Brandy from Beach Waves. You've all seen her at the warehouse, so wait for her signal for your turn to go."

Brandy held up her hand and waved. "I'll point to you when it's your turn."

"Let's get this parade started!" Kai announced, her voice carrying over the chatter of the crowd. She passed her clipboard to Brandy, who strode toward the front of the line and gave the mayor the signal.

Bennett began to drive slowly. "Off we go."

Ginger, Leo, Samantha, and Ivy waved to their fellow Summer Beach residents and visitors, and the crowd erupted in cheers.

Marina was thrilled with the response and support. But more than that, she thought of how much Summer Beach meant to her, the friendships she had discovered here, and the new life she'd created, both personally and professionally.

She was so grateful that Ginger was still in good health and had kept the Coral Cottage, even while she and Bertrand worked overseas. Summer Beach was home now, and Marina couldn't be happier.

Behind the mayor's car, floats began to roll forward. Each era of Summer Beach's history came alive, and people crowded onto the sidewalk to cheer them on.

Marina's heart was light, her spirit unburdened by earlier fears. Today was a day for Summer Beach residents to celebrate with their neighbors and welcome visitors. They were also honoring the foresight of those who came before and laid the groundwork for their sunny town by the sea.

"Here we go," Jack said, shifting the van into gear.

As Marina rode beside Jack in the procession down Main Street, she was filled with appreciation for her family, friends, and the enduring spirit of Summer Beach. Today, they were all united not only by history but also by a shared vision for their community's future—to keep Summer Beach a place they were proud to call home.

"They're calling out to you," Jack said, nodding toward people on the sidewalk.

"And to you," she said happily.

"Why wait a hundred years to celebrate like this again?"

Jack's words carried over the hum of the crowd, and Marina laughed.

22

*A*fter the parade, the crowd listened as the mayor addressed everyone from a podium at the end of Main Street near the beach.

Marina stood with Kai and Brooke, surrounded by their family. Heather, Ethan, and Blake were there, along with Axe, Brooke's husband Chip, and their three boys. Chip had his arm protectively around Brooke; they seemed closer now because of her pregnancy.

"Thank you all for joining us to celebrate one hundred years of Summer Beach history," Bennett said. "We have so many good times ahead, starting in just a few minutes with our old-fashioned burlap bag races."

Laughter rippled across the gathering.

Leo tugged on Jack's hand. "Can we do that, Dad?"

"How about you and Samantha be a team?" Jack suggested.

A flash of disappointment crossed the boy's face.

Jack leaned toward Marina. "I'm afraid I'd get hurt in the melee."

"I don't know," she said, grinning. "If other dads are out there…"

He made a face. "Okay, I get your point." He threw his arm around Leo. "On second thought, count me in, partner."

After the mayor finished, Ginger spoke, holding everyone's attention. She talked of her family's history in Summer Beach, also mentioning Marina's cafe and Kai's amphitheater with Axe. "The years I've spent in Summer Beach have been among the happiest in my life. And when the biography of my life is written, it will be my deepest pleasure to relive the memories."

People applauded, though Marina's lips parted in surprise. Ginger had always adamantly dismissed the idea of writing her story. Before she could say anything, Jack leaned in.

"Did you hear that?" His voice rose in excitement. "This might be my chance."

Jack had appealed to Ginger before, but she stood firm. Marina suspected many of her grandmother's experiences couldn't be shared because of classified information.

What had changed? Or did Ginger have another reason?

As if reading her mind, Ginger winked at her with a smile, confirming that she was up to something.

After Ginger finished speaking, the crowd thinned, moving to the food and carnival areas. Leo tugged Jack's hand, heading toward the games.

"What was that about your biography?" Marina asked Ginger when she joined them.

"Every person writes their life story," she replied with a slight Mona Lisa smile. "We'll talk about that later, dear."

Marina would have to wait. Ginger always did things on her terms and in her time. She nodded toward a photographer. "Looks like the mayor is waiting for you. I'll check on the food truck."

When Marina arrived, she saw a line of customers at the window—more than any other vendor had. Pleased, she circled around and stepped inside in the back. "How's it going?" she asked Cruise, who was making a panini and sweet potato fries.

"Great. The cookies and popcorn are hot today. We'll probably sell out. Good call on those."

"Need some help?" she asked.

"We've got this. Don't worry; we're not cutting any corners." Cruise grinned as he placed the panini on a paper plate. "I learned my lesson."

Marina was pleased to hear that. "Would you like Heather's help?"

"Let her spend time with Blake and Ethan," Cruise replied. "They stopped by a couple of minutes ago. Blake seems like a good guy. I approve."

Marina bumped fists with him. "Call me if you need me. And thanks for rocking this food truck."

"Listen to you," Cruise said, laughing. "Rock on, Chef."

Marina returned to watch Jack and Leo in the burlap sack race, and while they didn't win, they seemed to have the most fun.

Vanessa arrived with her husband, Noah, and they all talked while they watched. After the race, Leo joined his mother and stepfather, and they left for the carnival.

Jack turned to Marina. "Did you ask Ginger what she meant about her biography?"

"I tried, but you know Ginger. She likes to tease us; she'll tell us when she's ready."

"She's lived an amazing life," Jack said. "I have a feeling she has some surprises tucked away."

Marina's neck tingled at the thought. "I'm sure she does."

They talked while they strolled through the food area, sampling as they went.

"Fresh, homemade guacamole," Rosa called from her booth.

"We have to try that," Marina said. They still had time before she needed to return to the cafe for dinner. She ordered chips, salsa, and guacamole.

"Hey, you," Kai said, joining her.

Rosa served their order. With a playful glint in her eye, she poured three light green slushies and slid them across the table. "You should be celebrating your success," Rosa said. "Your favorites, on the house."

"They sure are." Marina tasted the frozen margarita. "That's yummy." She handed one to Jack and Kai. "Cheers on a successful centennial." She held up her cup, tapped Jack's, and turned to Kai.

"Um, sure. Cheers right back to you." Kai tapped their cups but didn't take a sip. Instead, she turned around. "Here comes Axe."

"Another one for him?" Rosa asked.

Kai darted a glance at Marina. "He can have mine."

Marina narrowed her eyes. It wasn't like Kai to turn down her favorite margarita on a warm summer day.

At once, she understood.

Axe joined them, and Kai hooked her arm through his, beaming.

"Do you have any news for us?" Marina asked, holding her breath. She hoped she was right this time.

"We sure do," Kai replied, letting out a squeal. "We just found out. We planned to wait until we were all together, but now you know. It won't be long until Brooke and I can arrange play dates with little ones."

Jack congratulated Axe, and they were all hugging when Brooke and Ginger joined them. Marina was so happy for her sisters, who were both ecstatic.

"Life has a way of working out," Ginger said, kissing them on the cheeks.

Marina clasped Jack's hand. "Indeed it does."

The cafe was busy that evening. Marina's staff arrived after they sold out at the centennial event. The younger families and teens stayed at the carnival, while others left for dinner in Summer Beach. The sun had set, and people were waiting to watch the fireworks.

"If you want to take a break, we can manage here," Cruise said.

"Thanks," Marina said, shrugging out of her chef jacket. She wore a light top under it.

She and Cruise had cooked together, with him following her lead. This was the busiest dinner they'd ever had, yet everything had gone smoothly. A satisfied feeling of success gathered in her chest, and she took a moment to enjoy it, appreciating all that she and her family through the generations had created on this shoreline.

Before she left, she slipped a narrow object into a pocket.

Stepping outside, she welcomed the cool evening air as it swept across her heated skin. She leaned against a palm tree, reflecting on the festival through a fresh lens of understanding. This day would remain in her memory as the canvas upon which the story of Summer Beach was drawn, with each stroke a color of its history, each hue a shade of its culture.

To her, the centennial was more than a milestone; it was the beginning of another chapter in a living narrative. Through the years ahead, lives would be transformed with each laugh shared, each bite savored, each memory created under these sunny skies.

She blinked, wiping a tear of happiness from her cheek. Her emotions had run the gamut today and remained close to the surface.

Jack strolled toward her, carrying a glass of red wine. Gently, he brushed her hair from her face. "Are you okay, love?"

"Never better, it seems." She smiled at him. "I'm happy you're here."

He handed her the glass. "Compliments of Ginger. A fine vintage Margaux she said you would like. Quite rare, like you." He followed her gaze. "Looks like everyone is enjoying themselves."

"That's all I set out to do," she said, feeling deeply grateful for where she was. "Make good food and provide a comfortable place to enjoy it by the beach."

Jack offered his arm. "Take a stroll with me?"

She smoothed her hand into the crook of his arm. "I'd like that." She brought the wine to her nose and then sipped, imagining the history captured in this ruby elixir.

They started for the beach, where moonlight illuminated white caps on the ink-blue ocean. When they reached the dunes, they slipped off their shoes and dug their toes into the sand, still warm from the day on top and cool beneath the surface.

A thin streak of light split the starry night, bursting into a kaleidoscope of color over the beach. Behind them, a cheer went up on the dining patio.

"What great timing you have," she said.

Smiling, Jack drew his arms around her shoulders and kissed her. "You're on to me, aren't you?"

"You still surprise me." She leaned into his embrace, savoring her wine and shivering with pleasure.

Jack caressed her face and kissed her forehead. "And you astonish me with your courage, your creativity. I'll never know how I got to be such a lucky guy."

"Give yourself some credit," she said, arching an eyebrow. "You were the total package. Handsome single dad, adorable child, overgrown puppy, great car. They write rom-coms about people like you."

Another firework shot into the sky, exploding into a silver waterfall.

Jack chuckled again. "And all along, I thought you only wanted me for my Pulitzer."

She poked him with faux exasperation. "Oh, enough of that. Don't you have something better to do with your life?"

"You bet I do," Jack said, a secret look on his face. "Remember that idea about filming discussions at the warehouse? Looks like there is strong interest in moving forward on it."

Marina's heart leapt with joy. "Oh, darling, I'm so happy for you."

"Life has never been better, Marina. Let's enjoy it." From his pocket, he withdrew a thin gold necklace with a glittering heart that rivaled a sky full of sparkles. "Happy first anniversary, my love. You have my heart for as many years as it beats. A hundred wouldn't be enough."

"Oh, this is beautiful, darling," she said, admiring the golden heart. His thoughtfulness meant so much to her. She kissed him, then lifted her hair. "Put it on for me?"

Jack clasped it, leaving a trail of kisses on her neck. "You bring it to life."

She shivered under his sweet touch. "And now, I have something for you." She reached into her pocket. "To inscribe your next book."

Jack's eyes lit at the gleaming fountain pen. "I've always wanted one of these, sweetheart. In fact, this very one. How did you know?"

"I have my sources," she replied, recalling her conversation with his sister. "Maybe that next book you write will be Ginger's."

"I should be so lucky. If not for renting the guest cottage to me when she did, we might not be standing here today." His voice held a husky note, and he slid his arm around her neck, bringing his lips to hers. "This is a day of celebration we'll never forget."

She savored his kiss. "A day among so many others we'll cherish."

Overhead, a firework burst with effervescent sparkles that light the night.

Marina offered him her wine, watching his mesmerizing blue eyes over the rim as he tested it. With their arms entwined, they stood watching the night sky, sipping wine from the same glass.

"What an exquisite life," she murmured, grateful for all they had endured, all they had overcome, and for what lay ahead in the story of their life yet to be written.

MORE FROM JAN MORAN

Thank you for reading *Coral Celebration*, and I hope you enjoyed the old-fashioned centennial party. Read on to discover *Coral Memories*, the final chapter of the Coral Cottage series, where Ginger Delavie takes center stage as Marina tries to unravel her grandmother's extraordinary life.

Receive a complimentary Summer Beach Welcome Kit by downloading an ebook or printable PDF from:

www.JanMoran.com/SummerBeachWelcomeKit

If you've read the *Seabreeze Inn* at Summer Beach series, you're also invited to join a special gala event in *Seabreeze Gala*, the next in that series.

And, discover a brand new branch of the family in *Beach View Lane*, and the latest, *Orange Blossom Way*.

Keep up with my new releases on my website and shop at JanMoran.com. Please join my VIP Reader's Club there to receive news about special deals and other goodies. Plus, find more fun and join other like-minded readers in my Facebook Reader's Group.

AUTHOR'S NOTE

More to Enjoy

If this is your first book in the Coral Cottage series, be sure to meet Marina when she first arrives in Summer Beach in *Coral Cottage*. If you haven't read the Seabreeze Inn at Summer Beach series, I invite you to meet art teacher Ivy Bay and her sister Shelly as they renovate a historic beach house in *Seabreeze Inn*, the first in the original Summer Beach series.

You might also enjoy more sunshine and international travel with a group of best friends in a series sprinkled with sunshine and second chances, beginning with *Flawless* and an exciting trip to Paris.

Finally, I invite you to read my standalone historical novels, including *Hepburn's Necklace* and *The Chocolatier*, a pair of 1950s sagas set in gorgeous Italy.

Most of my books are available in ebook, paperback or hardcover, audiobooks, and large print on my shop and from all major retailers. And as always, I wish you happy reading!

POPCORN FOUR WAYS RECIPE

In Coral Celebration, Marina prepares popcorn four ways to sell in her food truck at the centennial celebration. Whether you like savory rosemary and cheese flavors or sweet caramel and chocolate, there's a flavor for every taste.

Use your preferred method of preparing the popcorn, such as an air popper, microwave, or cooktop. These easy recipes can be made ahead or prepared hot for movie night. Enjoy!

Rosemary and Parmesan Cheese Popcorn

Ingredients:

½ cup (approx. 100g) unpopped popcorn kernels
3 tablespoons (45 ml) olive oil
2 tablespoons (approx. 6g) fresh rosemary, finely chopped
½ cup (approx. 50g) grated Parmesan cheese
Sea salt to taste

Instructions:

1. Pop the popcorn kernels and place the popcorn in a large bowl.

2. In a small bowl, mix olive oil and chopped rosemary.

3. Drizzle the rosemary oil over popped popcorn and toss to coat evenly.

4. Sprinkle grated Parmesan cheese over popcorn and toss again.

5. Add sea salt to taste and serve.

White and Dark Chocolate Drizzle Popcorn

Ingredients:

½ cup (approx. 100g) unpopped popcorn kernels
4 oz (115g) white chocolate (approx. ½ cup when chopped)
4 oz (115g) dark chocolate (approx. ½ cup when chopped)
Sea salt to taste (optional)

Instructions:

1. Pop the popcorn kernels and place the popcorn in a large bowl.

2. Use a microwave or a double boiler to melt white chocolate and dark chocolate separately.

3. Drizzle melted dark chocolate over the popcorn, then follow with white chocolate.

4. For a sweet and savory flavor profile, add sea salt to taste.

5. Allow the chocolate to cool and harden before serving.

Caramel Popcorn

Ingredients:

½ cup (approx. 100g) unpopped popcorn kernels
1 cup (approx. 200g) packed brown sugar
½ cup (approx. 115g) unsalted butter
¼ cup (60 ml) light corn syrup
½ teaspoon salt
½ teaspoon baking soda

Instructions:

1. Pop the popcorn kernels and place the popcorn in a large bowl.

2. In a medium saucepan, combine brown sugar, butter, corn syrup, and salt. Cook over medium heat until the mixture comes to a boil.

3. Boil for 5 minutes without stirring. Remove from heat and stir in baking soda.

4. Pour the caramel over the popcorn and stir to coat evenly.

5. Spread the popcorn on a baking sheet and bake at 250°F (120°C) for 45-60 minutes, stirring every 15 minutes.

6. Remove from oven and let cool before serving.

Three-Cheese Popcorn

Ingredients:

½ cup (approx. 100g) unpopped popcorn kernels
¼ cup (60 ml) melted butter
¼ cup (approx. 25g) grated Parmesan cheese
¼ cup (approx. 25g) grated Cheddar cheese
¼ cup (approx. 25g) grated Mozzarella cheese
Sea salt, to taste

Instructions:

1. Pop the popcorn kernels and place the popcorn in a large bowl.

2. Drizzle the melted butter over the popped popcorn and toss to coat.

3. Combine the Parmesan, Cheddar, and Mozzarella cheeses, then sprinkle over the popcorn.

4. Toss the popcorn to evenly distribute the cheese.

5. Add sea salt to taste and serve immediately.

ABOUT THE AUTHOR

JAN MORAN is a *USA Today* and a *Wall Street Journal* bestselling author of romantic women's fiction. A few of her favorite things include a fine cup of coffee, dark chocolate, fresh flowers, laughter, and music that touches her soul. She loves to travel, and her favorite places for inspiration are those rich with history and mystery and set against snowy mountains, palm-treed beaches, or sparkly city lights. Jan is originally from Austin, Texas, and a trace of a drawl still survives, although she has lived in Southern California near the beach for years.

Most of her books are available as audiobooks, and her historical fiction is translated into German, Italian, Polish, Dutch, Turkish, Russian, Bulgarian, Portuguese, and Lithuanian, and other languages.

If you enjoyed this book, please consider leaving a brief review online for your fellow readers where you purchased this book or on Goodreads or Bookbub.

To read Jan's other historical and contemporary novels, visit JanMoran.com. Join her VIP Readers Club mailing list and Facebook Readers Group to learn of new releases, sales and contests.

Made in the USA
Middletown, DE
14 January 2024

47854972R00137